MW01092935

HYSTERIA

LOLLY & LADY VANITY

ALI SEAY

Hysteria: Lolly & Lady Vanity © 2023 by Ali Seay. All rights reserved.

Grindhouse Press
PO BOX 540
Yellow Springs, Ohio 45387

Grindhouse Press logo and all related artwork copyright © 2023 by Brandon Duncan. All rights reserved.

Cover design by Squidbar Designs © 2023. All rights reserved.

Grindhouse Press #094
ISBN-13: 978-1-957504-04-9

This is a work of fiction. All characters and events portrayed in this book are fictitious and any resemblance to real people or events is purely coincidental.

No part of this book may be reproduced, stored in a retrieval system, or transmitted in any form or by any means, including mechanical, electric, photocopying, recording, or otherwise, without the prior written permission of the publisher or author.

Table of Contents

PROLOGUE

MY MOTHER WANTED TO NAME me Lolita. She was an avid reader and believed in unconventional names. My father put his foot down and said no. I became Lolly instead. I'm still not sure how I feel about that.

My sister's name was Snow because my mother's favorite fairy tale was *Snow White and the Seven Dwarves.* I guess my father had no issue with that because Snow White didn't tempt men old enough to know better. She just lived with seven short men and did their bidding.

My sister died—we presume—ten years ago. I'm twenty-one now. She'd be eighteen.

Sometimes I think I see her in a crowd. Sometimes I hear her talking to me when I'm asleep. Sometimes I wonder what I'd do if I found the man who took her from us.

1

THEN

"BUT WHAT IF THEY WON'T give it to me?"

My mother held a tissue over her mouth as she hacked and coughed. "Snow, honey, you're not picking up illegal drugs. You're picking up our prescriptions. I even called."

Snow twisted her sweater hem between her pale white fingers. Her complexion lived up to her name.

"But Ma—"

"Snow!"

My mother was losing her patience. We'd been sick with the flu for two long days. My temperature hovered at 103, hers a cool 101. Snow wasn't sick and neither was Daddy. But Daddy was at work and we weren't.

"All you have to do is go back to the counter. Mr. Rust is working. He's very nice. Remember him? He gives you lollipops."

I rolled my eyes. I was too sick to be diplomatic.

"Give him the money I gave you and he'll give you our medicine. There's an extra dollar there for a candy bar for you. Then come home. It's fine. Okay? It's only a block away."

My mother dissolved into a fit of hacking coughs and wheezes.

cion. I could be anyone. Hell, I could be Stanley.

Speaking of Stanley, little Mr. Fly had his attention.

I had a moment. An image in my head of me taking the big metal pole that read "Line Starts Here" and swinging for the fences against Stanley's head. Knocking everything out of him that preyed on little boys, that made him who he was. The monster he was.

I blinked. My head had actually snapped back as if I'd applied that force.

The woman behind me gave me a look and I gave her a look right back that made her face pucker up like an asshole.

The next person was called and the line shuffled forward.

Gotta love cold and flu season.

Stanley got to the front and there was some murmuring and some issues. He was asked to step to the side. Some kind of insurance glitch. Please have a seat, we're trying to sort it out.

I was almost to the front when little man came running up chasing a bouncy ball his mother must have gotten him from the quarter machines. He did it in a way only a sick little kid could. No shuffling, groaning staggering of an adult. The attempt to be normal and buoyant.

I watched the ball bounce, bounce, bounce—and then be snatched from the air by the clammy hand of Stanley.

The little boy stopped short. So suddenly he almost went down on his butt.

He giggled.

Stanley smiled.

The gray halo around his head seemed to throb.

I wanted to scream. I wanted to grab him by his ears and head butt him until his head rang.

"Demetri!" the boy's mother called. "Get your butt back here, boy."

Stanley had to force himself, I could see it. He held out the ball and the little boy took it. But not before Stanley closed his spidery fingers around the tips of Demetri's fingers. A rush to feel that baby skin? A buzz to feel that innocence under his touch?

My jaw ached from clenching my teeth.

"Ms. Valentine!"

My head whipped around so fast I felt dizzy.

"Sorry. Oh. Sorry," I mumbled, moving forward on unsteady feet.

3

THE PHARMACIST TYPED AND HUMMED and then clucked like a concerned hen.

"One of these is a controlled substance. The cough syrup with codeine. Do you have an adult with you?"

Any other day I'd have laughed. It happened so frequently. This time, after watching Spider Stanley and his greasy halo, I sighed. I dug my phone out of my back pocket and plucked my ID from the pocket attached to the back.

"I'm twenty-one," I said, sliding my driver's license across the counter to him.

He blinked, picked it up, studied it like it could be a fake. An elaborate ruse to get hold of a few milligrams of codeine.

"I'm terribly sorry. You just look so—"

"Very young. Yes. I know. It's fine. But I feel like crap so if I can get my prescription and go home, that'd be great."

"Of course." He went to the shelves and quickly found my bag. He rang me up and I paid with my bank card.

"Thanks."

"Feel better, Ms. Valentine."

4

IT RANG FOUR MORE TIMES as I stood there, heart pounding. My temples kept time.

Beneath me, the ruins of Stanley oozed into the rag rugs on the floor of his trailer.

There was an honest-to-God answering machine beep and I looked around. There, in a cascade of papers and dirty dishes on the tiny counter, was an answering machine.

"Stanley?"

She paused and I heard the crackle and pop of white noise around her.

"Stanley? It's Mom. Are you there?"

Another long pause. I became aware of the smell of the trailer. Unwashed man, dirty bedding, old food, and now, blood.

"It's Mom. I'm just checking in. The trip to Florida is good, but it's pretty hot here. Even though it's winter."

"Duh," I whispered.

"Wanted to make sure you were taking good care of Grace. If you don't, you know she'll claw my sofa to ribbons. I was hoping to catch you . . ."

I could feel the guilt coming through the phone. Though, if I had a raging pedophile for a son, I might go ahead and lay on a guilt trip too.

"Please be sure to feed her two times a day and give her some love. I hope you're . . ." She went silent again. "Being good. I'll see you day after tomorrow."

Click.

No "love you." No "call me back."

I think being good translated to not getting arrested or diddling little Sally in the alley.

I put a hand to my head and sighed.

"Now I have to go feed the cat for you, you piece of shit."

Lucky for me, as messy as Stanley's trailer was, he had a key rack on the wall by the door. I took a stab in the dark and chose the cat shaped key ring for the main house.

Snagging it, I poked my head out the door, looked around, and saw no one. I heard the hiss and rush of traffic not far off. The property backed up to a drop off to the Baltimore Beltway. It looked rural but the speed and light of traffic was only about a thousand feet away.

I hustled toward the house, hoping the whole way the key worked on the back door.

It did.

I entered the dim hush of the mud room.

"Grace?" I whisper-called.

Nothing.

I went to the kitchen, saw the cat's food mat with a bunch of kibble scattered around an almost empty bowl. The bulk store bag of kibble was right there on the floor. With or without Stanley, Grace wouldn't starve if she had any survival sense at all.

"Grace? Gracie?" I sing-songed. I wanted to pet the cat.

I'd just killed a man, but stroking a cat sounded divine. Like it might calm me down some.

I used the measuring cup in the bag to fill her bowl and suddenly she materialized. A black-and-smoke gray long-haired something. I didn't know much about cats.

She had one green eye, one brown.

"Hey there. I heard you might be hungry."

She sat on her bum and meowed at me.

"What's that? You need water, too? Of course."

14

I filled her water bowl and watched her ignore it stoically as she ate. I opened the fridge. Inside was a cloudy pitcher of iced tea, a bottle of apple juice, and a few cans of Coke.

I helped myself. Sat at the table and watched Grace eat.

She ate almost all the kibble but left a little around and in the bowl.

"Keeping your options open. Smart woman."

I rubbed my forehead vigorously, hoping it would help the headache. No luck.

I got up and opened the cabinets one by one until I found a bottle of generic pain reliever.

"Bingo!" I swallowed four of the rust-colored tablets with a swig of soda.

I sat back down at the table and hoped they worked soon. Grace hopped up on the seat next to me, then climbed onto the table.

Normally, I'd have found that gross, but Grace got a pass.

I stroked her soft head as she leaned into it and purred. "I killed your brother," I informed her.

She rubbed her muzzle against my hand.

"In my defense, he was a pervert and deserved it. Plus, something told me to."

Grace circled me, rubbing against my hand. She was a slut for attention.

"I don't know if it was God—'cause I don't believe in him—or divine intervention. I don't know. Do you believe in destiny?"

She just kept purring.

I gave her a few more pets and then laid my head down on my crossed arms. The table was old and hard and I didn't care. It felt luxurious to shut my eyes.

~

Something was pinning me down. I strained against it. I felt it shift, resettle. I strained against it again, and this time it let up with an offended meow.

Grace.

I opened my eyes.

Over the sink, an automatic nightlight shone.

"Shit."

The blue stove clock told me it was six-oh-eight. How long had I been asleep?

I sat up, my shoulders and neck screaming in stiffness. I

groaned.

The body. I had to deal with the body.

Grace had decided it was time to eat again. She insinuated herself into my lap and sat there staring at me like I was her new god.

I didn't want to turn the kitchen light on so I went to the bathroom right by the stairway. I flipped the light on and left the door open.

I filled Grace's bowl to the rim and took the bag and tore it down to the food line. This way, little miss thing could help herself until Stanley's mother was home.

I filled her bowl with water and then went in the bathroom and left the toilet seat up so there was another water source. As an afterthought, I left the kitchen sink dripping ever so slightly, barely noticeable but enough for Grace if she needed it.

I wiped down the table and everything I could remember I'd touched with the inside of my sweater.

"Murder, cat sitting, cleaning. I do it all," I whispered.

Then I locked the back door and pulled it shut behind me. I made sure I had the key in my pocket to put it back on Stanley's key peg.

I had to deal with the body and then I could go home and sleep for real.

5

I DUG HIM A GRAVE. It was shallow, but a grave nonetheless.

I had dragged him to the edge of the property on a painter's tarp I'd found in the trailer closet. I pushed him into the depression with my foot and kicked the dirt back over him. Lights from the beltway lit it well enough for me to see but not well enough for me to be seen.

I hoped.

Next, I kicked some leaves over the spot. I dragged the tarp to the edge of the property and dropped it halfway down the hill. Within a day or so the wind would carry it down to the speeding cars and big rigs and God knew where it would end up.

Satisfied I was done, I stumbled back toward the house, passed his trailer with the door hanging open, and made my way to my car.

The neighborhood still looked deserted. I wondered how many people lived here. A lot of these streets were more than fifty percent empty houses on the market.

My neighborhood was dying.

I drove home, grabbed a bottle of water, took off my clothes and got into bed. I was too tired to shower the death off.

6

THEN

I ROLLED OVER ON THE sofa just in time to see the door shut.

My mother, on the other sofa, sighed.

"That girl," she said. "Afraid of her own shadow."

I shrugged, suddenly feeling very defensive of Snow. "She's just a kid. She's used to me doing this stuff with her."

"Or for her," my mother said.

"Sometimes."

A game show chattered in the background, accented by my mother's hacking cough and my rattling one. We were a hell of a backup band.

I dozed off.

"—time is it?"

"What?"

"What time is it?" My mother sounded like she might have dozed off too.

"Twelve fifteen."

"What time did Snow leave?"

"I don't know."

She was quiet. The game show returned, loud and jangly. It was suddenly much more grating.

My mother sat up straight. A flurry of tissues fell off her quilt and she reached out a hand to steady herself.

"Dizzy," she said.

"Move slower," I advised.

"I think she's been gone too long," my mother said.

I heard the fear in her voice then and my own fear stabbed me straight through like an ice pick.

My mother stood slowly, her quilt puddled at her feet. I sat up too, her worry infecting me.

Dizziness hit me and I put my head down for a moment.

"I think she went about a half an hour ago. We were halfway through *The Wheel*."

I blinked. She was right.

"That's only a half an hour."

"The pharmacy is a block and a half away," she snapped. "You know that."

I did. When Snow and I went to buy candy it only took about five minutes to get there and five minutes back. Most of our trip was spent on the selection of said candy.

My mouth was suddenly dry. "Maybe the pharmacy is very busy," I said. "It's cold and flu season." I laughed a little at that. Obviously it was. We were both currently at the flu's mercy.

My mother grabbed the phone off the end table and started to dial, hung up, tried again.

"Yes, hi. This is Joanna Valentine. My daughter Snow was coming to pick up a prescription for me and her sister Lolly. Have you se— Yes, that's right. She did? Okay. Thank you."

I could hear it then. The incredible blind panic in her voice.

My stomach rolled over again and I had to run to the bathroom once more.

My mother shouted. "She left twenty minutes ago, according to him. That's wrong, Lol. Wrong!"

When I came out, she was already on the phone with the police.

7

NOW

"THEY FOUND MY SHOE IN the gutter."

I opened my eyes.

Snow stood there, hiding her head in the corner of my room. Her hair was dark to my light. Her body petite to my tall. My mother had called us Mutt and Jeff.

"Snow?"

"By the time they finally got up there to check on me, he'd taken me. My shoe was in the gutter, the prescription for you guys dumped in the trash bin on the corner."

I swallowed hard. My head throbbed, my eyes were blurry, my throat was full of razor blades.

I wiped my eyes, hoping this was a hallucination.

It had to be.

Snow had been gone and/or dead for a decade.

"Do you know what he did to me?"

I shook my head, feeling wetness on my face. I was crying.

No. I didn't. No one did. Or if there even was a he. Or if she was dead, alive, being held captive. Did she have amnesia? Was she a sex slave? Was she a sex worker in some other city now?

I sobbed.

"You need to fix this. Fix these people. Stop them."

I nodded, wiping my nose with my arm. Snot smeared up from my wrist to my shoved-up shirt sleeve.

I'd been sweating in my sleep. I could smell my own body and the copper tang of Stanley's blood on me.

This wasn't a dream. None of it.

"Fix it," Snow said.

She started to turn and my brain yammered at me.

Dontlookdontlookshesdeadhasbeenitllbeawfuldontlook

I sneezed.

I wiped my eyes and realized she was gone.

It was eleven fifty-seven. I'd slept right through the night. All morning. And the state of my clothes, hands, and shoes over on the floor, told me my adventures with Stanley had been very real. And I needed to shower. Immediately.

~

The shower just made me tired all over again. I found an old envelope of instant soup in the cabinet and poured hot water into it. That and a handful of stale crackers were lunch. I swallowed my antibiotic, took a shot of my antiviral, then took a shot of my cough syrup, thought about it, and took other. As an afterthought, I took some Tylenol. The worst of the fever seemed to be gone, but it sure as shit couldn't hurt.

I grabbed a bottle of water and a warm can of Coke and headed back to bed. I almost made it but my phone started ringing. An ominous weird horn sound that signaled my mother calling.

I groaned. I couldn't. But I had to.

My dad had left about a year after Snow had gone missing. Neither could forgive the other and the marriage turned into a sideshow. I stayed out of it, going out with friends, drinking, smoking pot, and trying to forget I'd ever had a sister.

He moved to North Carolina when I was thirteen and started a whole new family. I haven't heard from him since I was fifteen.

I had to take my mother's call because, with the exception of her mediums, fortune teller, and woo-woo crunchy yoga friends, I was all she had.

"Hey, Ma," I said, followed by a long string of strangled coughs. Between being upright and the steam of the shower, my lungs were trying to crawl out of my body.

21

8

MY BLADDER WOKE ME UP early. Seven fifteen I staggered to the bathroom, peed for a year, and then went to take my meds. I felt better. But still weak as hell.

I put the kettle on and prepped the French press for coffee. The coffee sounded good, but we'd see what would happen when it actually hit my gut.

It could be a shit show. Literally.

I only had a few more doses of the antiviral. I was told to finish it even when I felt better. I'd do as told.

Can the flu, antivirals, and childhood trauma turn you into a killer? Asking for a friend.

I was more freaked out about how not freaked out I was about ending Stanley than by actually ending Stanley.

I wondered if anything had dug him up? Carried parts of him down to the beltway below or if he was there, under the leaves, dreaming of little boys?

I shivered, poured myself a cup of coffee, and doctored it. The first sip was heaven. Fuck, I hoped it stayed down.

I turned on the TV and flipped to the local news. I waited, wondering if anything about a dead child molester would show up. After my first cup of coffee, I figured if it was going to, it was certainly way down on the list of importance. Considering we'd already seen a live news report on not only the upcoming cat show but of a man who "adopted" old Christmas ornaments for his Christmas extravaganza.

I turned off the TV, plugged in my laptop, and booted it up. The battery was nearly dead.

On my Facebook feed, I winged past all kinds of nonsense and eventually clicked on **What's Up 21206?**, the local thread where everyone bitched about everything. I'd started following because a few of these women were obsessive about the local kiddie diddlers.

Suddenly, that was a good thing for me. I had a taste for Stanley 2.0 and had zero guilt about it.

"I'm a serial killer," I said aloud.

But I wasn't sure if I was. I didn't think so. Not yet.

My phone reminded me I had a voicemail and I listened to it.

Rich said, "Hey, it's me. Just checking in. Haven't heard from you for a while . . ." Long pause. "I know we're not a thing-thing, but we're kind of a thing." A chuckle. "A weird thing. But it works for us." Additional long pause. "Anyway, I just wanted to know if we could get together soon or thought maybe you met someone, in which case you could just tell me—" Big sigh. "Call me when you can. Sorry I rambled. Hope everything is okay."

"Everything's okay." I clicked the phone off and started scrolling **What's Up 21206?**.

It seemed the most recent target of Michelle and Robin, the women who seemed to track everyone who'd ever done anything, was a woman.

"That's interesting."

I poured another cup of coffee and put sugar and cream in it. The first was staying down. So far, so good.

Michelle wrote: This woman was accused of molesting children and she's running a daycare!!! OMG

Robin responded: How is that possible? Someone should call the police. What is wrong with this country?!

Michelle: They have!!!! No help.

Robin: Really? That's insane. Someone should call again. Someone should protest!

Michelle: I've called every day. They just keep saying they're

25

"looking into it." Well, look into it faster! OMG, I can't even.

Robin: That's disgusting.

I read on, sussing out the woman in question was about two miles away. One of them had helpfully posted her picture.

I studied Natalie. She looked like a normal, overweight, unhappy, bland woman who was just waiting for some excitement in her life.

I went to the page for her daycare. Bright Mornings Daycare. There were pictures of happy playing children. None of her. It was a public page so I saw the comments from Michelle and Robin and other people in an uproar.

Admin had not responded.

I wondered if she had a halo. I wondered if she did what they said. I wondered if she deserved to die.

~

She had a halo. Darker gray than Stanley's with flecks of puke color in it. I wondered if that was because she was a woman and we're supposed to, more than anyone, be their protectors. The children.

"It's unusual not to have the child at these meetings," Natalie said to me.

I bet.

"Well, Charlie gets a little nervous in new situations." I chose Charlie because I read her main prey were boys. "I figured I'd come alone first."

I offered her my cell phone where a little boy beamed at the camera. His hair was what my mother would have called corn silk. He had big blue eyes, a few little freckles over his perfect nose. Of course, it was a screenshot from the internet, but she didn't know that.

He was perfect.

Perfect bait.

She practically salivated. My stomach churned, that coffee taking a turn for the worse.

"He's lovely. Gorgeous," she said.

A little girl ran in and saw us talking and immediately backpedaled. No interrupting, no asking for snacks, no babbling, just an immediate about-face.

Interesting.

"He is. The light of my life. A little shy. He's on the spectrum, so he's not highly verbal. Barely talks to me, and I'm his mom. Has a hard time sometimes explaining things that are happening around him."

Her eyes lit up. A victim who'd have trouble tattling or explaining what happened to him? Sign her up!

"I see. That shouldn't be a problem at all."

I wondered how she even had *any* kids in her care. Were the parents simply computer illiterate, uninformed, or the worst—the ones that refused to believe the person in their life was capable of such atrocities. At the expense of their own children, no less.

I had no fucking clue. And I didn't care. I just wanted to wipe that halo out and move on.

"When could we meet?" she asked. "To see if we're compatible."

I shrugged as if I hadn't a care in the world. "He's with his grandma now." I lowered my voice. "I'm a single mother. His father isn't in the picture."

She patted my leg. "I thought you looked way too young. I see now," she said. But her face said more. Her face said I was someone who will be frazzled, distracted, and less inclined to pay hyper attention to her. A woman more prone to trusting her implicitly.

"I could bring him back later. After all these kids leave. It would be better for him, at first. You understand . . ."

"Of course, of course." She started to rattle off what I'd need to know. The weekly fee, the procedure for drop off, pick up, and if he was sick.

Since I didn't need to know any of it, I tuned out, waiting for the lull in her voice.

"Great. That all sounds good," I said as my stomach gave a warning gurgle. I glanced at my phone. "I have to get going for now. What time should I come back?"

"Six?"

"Six it is."

She shook my hand and I hoped I was still contagious. "I'll see you then."

"Yes, you will," I said with a little finger wave like a young single mother who'd just hit the jackpot of childcare. "Can't wait!"

It was true. I couldn't wait. But first I had to get home before I shit my pants.

"Because I can. Because I can see you for what you are." I nodded at the halo but realized she didn't even know it was there. "Because it's a person like you who ruined my family."

She turned to bolt and I swung. I played softball in my youth. Mainly because my dad was a coach and Snow pestered me until I agreed. The thing is, even when you hate something and don't want to do it, occasionally, you're good at certain things anyway.

I was a really good batter.

She went down hard. I heard something hit the floor, and then a skitter and bump. A tooth. She'd come down face first, mouth open.

"Oh, that's gotta hurt."

She started to crawl. This was for Snow. My mom. My dad— that fuck. He left because of the pain. I knew that. I still hated him for it every day. But I knew.

This was for the little kids she'd hurt and the ones she intended to.

The shovel made a thud followed by a hollow *pong!* sound as it skittered off the back of her skull and scraped the old, warped linoleum around her.

There was a flat spot on the back of her skull.

Interesting.

I hit her again. And again. There was a crack and another noise—this time a *bong!*—and the head of the shovel bounced off the kitchen floor. My arms shook and my neck ached. I had a slab of pain from shoulder to shoulder. Not only was I using muscles I hadn't used in forever, but I was just coming off being sick for many days.

The fucking flu, man. It will wear you out.

She was still advancing. Way slower than she probably wanted. But she gave it her all. No one could deny Natalie was a stubborn cunt.

I followed along. It wasn't hard. I raised the shovel, started to bring it down, and slipped in her blood. I went down on my ass. My teeth clacked together, and the shovel whacked my ankle painfully hard. I saw stars for a second and sat there, stunned, taking inventory of my body.

She was struggling to her knees, breathing raggedly, her head draped with rivulets of blood. It reminded me of those elaborate headpieces flappers had worn in the 20s. Like if she shook her head, a thousand little red beads would start to dance.

I giggled.

She turned, her face a ruin, her front tooth missing, another broken off. I saw her notice the wall phone and thought, *Well fuck, who even has a land line anymore?*

Apparently, Natalie.

She reached for it, faltered, reached for it again. Her fingertips brushed the blue plastic slimline. That snapped me out of it. I got hold of the shovel again and gave an awkward swing.

It was shit. In a softball game it would have been laughable. But she was already half down and out and bleeding. The end of the shovel head clipped her chin and snapped her head back.

I tried to stand, but my ankle gave and I screamed.

"Fuck you! Now look what you've done!"

She stared at me, stunned. Her face pale but for the splashes of blood, her hair in ruins. Air whistled in and out of her broken mouth.

"Me?" she asked, confused.

"Yes! You! Who else?"

Her eyes fluttered like she was going to hit the ground. Finally. So I clocked her again. Harder this time.

Her head lolled. The edge of the shovel head sliced her cheek open. A wide slit from the edge of her mouth up into her cheek.

"Half a Glasgow smile," I said.

She looked at me as if to say, *What?*

I shook my head. "Never mind. Just fucking go down, will you?"

She tried again. It was heroic really. She reached for the phone. Her fingers tipped against it and it jostled up and off. Then it swung down, hitting her in the head. It bounced away from her mutilated noggin, swinging wildly back and forth at the end of its tether.

The physical exhaustion had me practically punch drunk. The look on her face when that phone hit her was priceless and giggles rippled through me. I sounded like something you'd hear in the background of a movie about an insane asylum.

But I wasn't crazy, I was simply sick and touched by the divine, apparently. Doing my holy job of cleaning up the world for girls like my sister.

Somehow, God, if there was one, had reached out to me via antivirals, cough syrup, and flu sweats.

Far be it from me to ignore my duty.

ALI SEAY

She went down and I got up. Not to my feet—to my knees. I shuffled toward her, panting, trying to catch my breath. I was sweating now, horribly so. Cold, clammy, it coated my skin beneath my shirt. I knew if I stuck my hand under there, I'd draw it away slick and cool.

On my knees, I hovered over her. "Tell me," I said.

"Tell you what?" Blood flew out of her mouth, speckling her face.

"Tell me you did it. Tell me you're a monster."

"I'm not." She waved one hand weakly at me.

"You are. I can see it in your eyes."

"Not—" Her breathing was ragged.

"Tell me the truth and I might spare you."

She stared up at me. One pupil was bigger than the other.

I took a faux swing at her and she sputtered, "Okay! Okay. I've done it. I'm trying to get better. I've been doing good."

My stomach turned and I thought the little bit in there was going to come up.

"Better?"

"Yeah, I've done better. In the last six months I've only fucked up once. But that little one, Alex, he just makes it so eas—"

I brought the shovel down blade first into the disgusting hole of her mouth. Her face opened up like a giant book, her tongue sliding to one side.

Well, that had felt good.

10

I WAS SHAKING. HARDER NOW. I had to go. I didn't want to pass out here and be found.

But I couldn't go. I had to deal with her body. I had to bury her or something.

I sat on my ass and scooted back against the oven to catch my breath.

I could leave her. God knows, the messages on **What's Up 21206?** and the messages on her very own Facebook page would give the police plenty of suspects. I wasn't on her page, I wasn't on **21206?**, and I wasn't a parent.

I wouldn't even be on their radar.

However . . . kids and their parents would be showing up in the morning. Some of these kids had been through enough. Looking at the face of Miss Natalie all opened up like the worst present ever was bad.

"Think. Think." I took my shirt sleeve and wiped down the handle of the shovel. It was the only thing I'd touched.

I studied her small, modest kitchen. A stack of little plastic snack bowls, a superstore-size box of Goldfish crackers, a jug of apple

11

SOMEONE WAS BANGING ON MY door. I sat up, felt dizziness club me over the head, and stayed there until it passed.

I was cold. I'd been sweating all night.

Tail end of the flu, my ass. I'd supposedly been almost done when I saw the doc. That was two days ago? Three? Four? I couldn't tell.

The knocking had stopped. Maybe they'd gone away.

I stood slowly and the knocks started again.

"Jesus! I'm coming!" I shuffled out of the bedroom and down the hall. I peeked out my door and saw my mother standing there.

"Oh fuck. I can't do this," I hissed.

"Lolly! I know you're here. I saw your car down in the parking lot. Open up."

I opened the door and stared at her. "Hi, Ma."

My mother took me in. It only took her a moment to do a head-to-toe once over as is the way of mothers. "You look awful."

"Thanks. Come on in." I did a sweep of my arm and my shoulder muscles shrieked at the exaggerated movement. Ugh.

"You need to let some light in. It'll kill the germs."

I doubted that.

She walked around flinging up shades and opening the curtains that were already in the apartment when I rented it.

"Did you just come to blind me?"

"No. Of course not. Don't be silly. I'll make you some tea."

She hustled into my kitchen in her black leggings, oversize sweatshirt, and running shoes. My mother runs. My mother lifts weights. My mother goes to mediums and watches them on TV and listens to podcasts about the dead. My mother is a whirlwind.

I heard her put the kettle on and then her furious rummaging through my cabinets.

"Lolly!"

"What?" I went to her slowly. As slowly as humanly possible.

"You have no food. That's why you're sick."

"Yes. I have the flu because of my lack of food in the house and my closed curtains. I'm pretty sure it's a viral situation."

She sighed, put two plain tea bags in mugs, found a bottle of crystalized honey and, after disappearing from the waist up into my fridge, found a bottle of lemon juice in a fake plastic lemon.

She set about making the tea.

I waited.

"The day after tomorrow is the anniversary of your sister's disappearance."

"I'm sorry." I didn't know what else to say.

"I just wanted to see you and say that I keep dreaming about her and Miriam says she's around us. That she's feeling vindicated for some reason. And that's good. That's why she keeps contacting me in my dreams."

I managed to not roll my eyes at Miriam the Medium. My mother seemed to have a fleet of them. I lost track sometimes.

"I'm glad. That makes you happy, obviously."

She nodded. "Do you think about her?"

"All the time. Especially lately."

Not a lie.

She patted my arm. "Good."

My mother finished the tea, presented me with my mug, and we sat and talked for a few minutes. She blurted, "There was a fire not far from me last night!"

I waited.

"A daycare no less!"

"Terrible," I said, seeing, in my mind's eye, Natalie's face splitting open like a rotten pumpkin.

"Thank goodness none of the kids were there. It was just the woman who ran it at home. I guess that's the silver lining."

"Yes, it is."

She rambled about other things—a new guy she was dating, maybe adopting a dog, her latest Reiki session, and what did I want for Christmas.

Then she left.

I finally exhaled. My mother is a force of nature.

"I remember you, Snow," I said. "I just don't need psychic mediums to talk to you. I just fucking talk to you."

I crawled back into bed and slept until late afternoon.

13

I WAS STARTING TO THINK having to find your own murder weapon at the scene technically made the murder spontaneous.

Right?

Dick led the way and I felt my first prickle of fear. It was distant and dull, but it was fear. So low key it was almost just worry, but still.

What if there was no weapon? What if we weren't alone?

I walked up the rickety wooden steps to the painted porch on his heels. I hung back just a little to get a glimpse inside the home.

A shambles. That's what it looked like.

A sagging sofa, barely any furniture, a blanket on that sofa (did he sleep there?), an old TV so deep and big it had to be twenty years old on an equally aged stand. No pet waiting to greet us.

I hesitated, just like any thirteen-year-old girl would. "Is your wife home?" I asked. "Will I be bothering her?"

Valid question.

His forehead wrinkled and he tried to fake a smile. "My wife is living in South Carolina with a guy named Mateo and my dog."

I wanted to laugh. I pressed my lips together.

"I'm sorry."

"It's fine. Come on, I'll get you a drink."

I bet. Spiked with something, no doubt.

"Can we walk around outside for a bit. I haven't been out much the last few weeks. I was in bed sick. It feels good to move around."

He looked disappointed but nodded. When wooing an underage girl, one had to practice restraint, no doubt.

"Sure, let's walk around back. There's a gazebo out there. I bet you'd like that."

We walked around the side of the house and I scanned the ground and my surroundings as we went. Sadly, no hammer, no shovel. But there was hope. There was always hope. Dick wasn't a neatnik with his home so there had to be shit lying around I could use in a pinch.

He unlatched a sagging gate. Everything in his life was sagging, apparently. The backyard was enormous. It didn't fit the tiny house at all. There was a—you guessed it—sagging wooden gazebo with some cheap plastic outdoor furniture inside. There was a pool. The pool was dark and murky and I stared hard. If I gazed hard enough into the shadows, I felt like I could see inky figures moving out there, climbing from the water, stalking toward us.

I shook my head and the image cleared.

"You okay?" He touched my arm and I had to suppress the urge to smack his hand.

"Fine. Just got a chill. Do you swim a lot?"

Of course he didn't swim a lot. Alligators could live in that fucking pool. It was clearly useless. Even illuminated by nothing more than the neighborhood streetlights, you could see it was neglected, dirty, and downright swamp-like.

He snorted. "Not lately. I haven't had time to work on the pool for a while."

Ten or fifteen years maybe.

Around the pool was a ring of rocks. I wandered like I was aimless, but I wanted to be close to them. About the size of large baking potatoes but organically shaped. Perfect to palm in a pinch. Say that three times fast.

"You okay?" He was putting on his concerned face. His daddy face.

I shuffled my feet, realizing how much the winter wind was biting through my fleece pajama pants. My car keys were in my jacket pocket. My phone in the other. I had both pockets zipped so I didn't lose anything.

How was this going to go down? How would it happen? And while we were at it, why now? Was it the drugs? Had I snapped? Why now?

Ten years, big sis. A landmark . . .

Snow's voice in my head. I had forgotten what she sounded like until that moment. No way I actually heard it, and yet I did.

"Just cold," I said.

He pulled me in for a hug. It was gross. Had I been thirteen, I'd have been freaked out. Had I been a thirteen-year-old with a shitty home life, I have no idea how I would've been. I had parents who cared. At least until Snow disappeared. Even then, I still had one. And neither of them neglected me or pawned me off. I think, sometimes, my father blamed me for her disappearance. I was sick too. I usually would have been the one to go.

It should have been me.

"You can relax here. It's fine." He pulled back, looked down at me. His breath smelled like mothballs. "Gosh, you're pretty."

I tried to move out of his grasp and the whole scene shifted. His face went from faux concern to predatory. His fingers dug into my skin. His arms were like a vice. Dick was much stronger than his doughy appearance indicated.

I wiggled again and sneezed—fake but very hard—into his face. He reflexively let me go. But then he reached for me again.

"Leave me alone," I said, weakly. Another small step back.

"Oh, don't give me that. You knew what this was about when you came here with me."

"What is it?"

He took a swipe at me like an angry bear and I managed to dodge it.

"Like you're a virgin. I can look at you and tell that's bullshit."

It didn't take much to go from nice, caring night manager to nasty dude. Interesting.

"I don't know what you're talking about. I'm only thirteen."

A sneer. Now he was edging toward me, like a deer hunter stalking his target. Thinking I wouldn't notice his micro motions.

"I think you do. I've been with little whores younger than you. You all act so innocent and afraid, but really, you're laughing. Loving how it makes men feel."

Eww.

He grabbed at me then.

I ducked, stooped quickly, grabbed a rock. I had a moment where it slipped from my hand and I thought I was fucked. My fingers scrambled and I finally managed to snag it. He had hold of me already, but it wasn't tight because of the angle.

I came up fast and struck out with the rock. It clipped him on the chin. Not hard. Just hard enough to piss him off and snap his teeth together.

He snagged my jacket front and yanked. I went up on my toes, scrambling. The rock trapped nearly between us. I experienced my first real jolt of panic.

Had I made a terrible mistake?

"What the fuck, little girl? You think you can hurt me?"

I stared into his shit brown eyes, smelling his grandma's attic breath. Was it him? A man like him? Had someone like this—this vile, this horrible—taken my baby sister? Were her last days like this? With a man like this. Or worse, were her days *still* like this?

That thought did me in. Considering her in prolonged agony. A captive. My insides ripped like someone had drawn down a zipper. I hurt. I hurt so bad there was no way to contain my rage.

He smiled at me. "I didn't think so."

After Snow went missing, my mother made me take self-defense. Jiu jitsu, Taekwondo, kickboxing. I was bad at all of it. Once, I had an instructor yell out in class, "This isn't ballet class, Lolly! Stop pointing your toe!"

But the knee to the groin thing? Any monkey can do that.

I remembered one thing in particular. Grab him. Keep him close.

I grabbed him with my free hand and jutted my knee up at his crotch as hard as I could. I'm fairly certain I did indeed point my toe, but who cares?

The air bled out of him in a single rush like a balloon being slit open. He dropped down a few inches and I took the chance to raise the rock, grab it with both hands, and bring it down on his head. There was a crunch, not unlike good old Stanley's noggin.

He went down to his knees.

"You disgust me," I snarled.

He opened his mouth in a sneer, no doubt to say something obnoxious. Guys like him didn't hardly ever realize when they were losing the fight. Guys like him always had something to say. Nice guys like Dick.

"You are a shit stain on humanity. You are a hemorrhoid of a human. You are a boil on the ass of society."

I brought my knee up into his face this time. His teeth drove into my knee. Hard. I felt them puncture my skin. Felt the blood run. And I fucking loved it.

I did it again. And then again.

He gagged, lolling away from me, but I followed him.

The skin over my kneecap was screaming but I took another shot right to his mouth. A tooth was stuck in my pant leg. Slobber leaked out of his mouth. I brought the rock down, crushing it against his skull and shifted and jabbed it forward into his already fucked up mouth.

"You are a freak. A sin. A fucking monster."

I pushed him back with my foot and was grateful I hadn't gone out in my slippers. I'd actually put on my sneakers.

He went down stiffly, stunned by this thirteen-year-old's random attack—both verbal and physical.

I kicked him in the mouth.

God, that fucking felt good.

I couldn't escape the image of my little sister, so cute, so sweet, so annoying, so awkward, with someone like this. Trapped. Held captive. What had he done to her? What had he made her endure?

Another kick. A third. The wet rasp of him trying to draw breath hit my ears and it was music. Angels singing. The best god damn thing I'd ever heard.

I kept kicking him until he was down on his back, hands waving weakly. I held the rock but didn't need it anymore. I knew that.

He lay there, staring up at me. One eye half shut from a blow. His teeth, simple broken stumps in his mouth. He licked his lips and gagged.

"Please."

"Please what?"

"Stop," he gasped. "Just go. I won't call the cops."

"Please stop?" I confirmed.

He nodded, hands waving uselessly.

"You want me to stop hurting you?"

Another nod.

"I wonder how many times your victims said those exact

words?"

His eye went wide. The other was hopelessly swollen.

"I bet they asked that all the time, didn't they?"

He didn't answer. He pedaled his hands and feet like he was trying to crab walk away from me, but being flat on his back, that was impossible.

"I bet you didn't, did you, *Dick*? I bet you didn't stop when they asked. Right?"

He stared at me, looked away, looked back again.

I put my foot right over his face. Hovering. So close he could smell his own blood on my sole. "Answer me or I will stomp you until you choke on your own fucking tongue."

"No . . ." he sobbed. He drew the word out like a wolf warbling at the moon.

"I didn't think so," I said.

I found a surge of energy somewhere. And I hopped hard, using that energy, and landed with both feet in the bloody cavern of his mouth. Smashing his face to a pulp, feeling his jaw bones crunch, his tongue a mushy mass beneath my feet.

I stood there in the aftermath for a moment, and then moved. A light rain was starting. I'd forgotten it was supposed to rain at all.

I stepped off his face, my feet slick on the pebbled cement around the pool.

"I appreciate you supplying a burial ground." I bent and grabbed his ankles, careful to only touch the cuffs of his pants and not his boots. Not that I thought any chance of fingerprints existed, but better safe than sorry.

I dragged him slowly toward the bayou swamp of a pool. I yanked and tugged and dragged. He was a heavy motherfucker and I was much smaller than him. Not to mention still technically sick.

I got him to the edge and had to put my hands on my knees and catch my breath.

Finally, realizing I wasn't going to feel much better any time soon, I pushed him in. He went in slowly, sort of sliding into the water in slow motion. It reminded me of watching footage of alligators slipping into the water because they spotted a possible meal.

Before I forgot, I walked back to where I'd ended the monstrosity that was Dick and grabbed the rock. I walked it back and dropped it in after him.

There was no sign of him or the rock. I used my phone flashlight to be sure. Nothing. The water was as dark as beef stew and full of leaves and debris. It would be a while before anyone found him.

I passed his Bronco on the way out of the driveway. I used my sleeve to wipe down the handles because I couldn't remember if I'd touched them. I grabbed my food trash and took it with me. A few blocks away, I shoved it in someone's trash that waited on the curb for morning pickup.

It took me quite a while to walk back to the RoFo. I was grateful the lot had been full because I'd parked down on the side street. If for some reason any video feed pointed a finger at me, I'd simply say I'd left and driven home.

Let them prove otherwise.

14

I SLEPT LIKE THE DEAD again after taking my final shot of antiviral. I swallowed my enormous antibiotic using my cough syrup. My shoulders ached, my neck muscles too. The rock had been heavier than I'd thought. It was just a matter of me being fueled with adrenaline and hatred.

"I love you, Snow. I hope this helps," I told my sister as I felt the codeine hit me like a cotton-wrapped fist.

Somewhere in the middle of the night I had to pee. I got up, walked past my sister where she stood in the corner, dressed exactly as she had the day she disappeared.

She didn't seem upset. She seemed content there in the corner, like one of those creepy dolls that appears to be hiding its face against the wall.

I went back to bed thinking at least I knew where she was now.

~

I put the pillow over my pounding head and held it there, trying to zone back out into blissful sleep.

Pound-pound-pound.

It wasn't my head. It was the door.

50

My mother. Who else would it be at—
I rolled over and looked at the cable box on my dresser. 11:23?
Hopefully it was morning.
Since I saw sun, I figured it was a safe bet.
"Oh my God." I rolled to my side and slowly forced myself into
a sitting position. The flu was still twisting my bones while I slept.
Even though, officially on the "upswing," I woke feeling like I'd
been curled in a tight ball all night and all my limbs had gotten stuck
that way.
More pounding.
"Hold on!" I tried to bark, but my voice broke and I dissolved
into a hacking coughing fit that made me feel like I was going to
hock up a lung.
"Jesus, Ma. No need. This is ridiculous."
I shuffled past the corner where my sister had lurked in the middle of the night. She was nowhere to be found. Chased off by sun-
light and sanity, no doubt.
"You don't have to deal with her crazy shit," I said to Snow.
Maybe she'd hear me. "She's all love and light one week and fuck
the world and burn it down because her baby was taken the next.
She's been that way for a decade now."
I sighed. Halfway to the front door I wanted to lie back down
and sleep some more. My body hurt not just from the flu but from
all the strenuous activity lately.
No one tells you how much physical effort murder takes.
I shut my eyes and tried again, "Hold on! I'm coming!"
The banging stopped.
Thank fucking god.

15

I'D BEEN EXPECTING MY MOTHER. Instead, Rich stood there. My on again off again fuck buddy. Once a serious boyfriend but that didn't work so now he's just a person in my life. A guy. Who wanted to be more again.

He cocked his head. The searing sunlight backlighting him like he was going toward the light in a movie. Or I was.

"Lolly?"

"That's me," I said, suddenly tired all over again.

Rich is needy. Rich needs to talk about things. Rich needs to overexplain himself. Rich needs to know how I feel. Rich needs me to know how he feels. It's one of the reasons we were off again.

"You okay?"

He hovered there in the doorway, unsure if he should come in. If he *could* come in.

"I am. Mostly."

"I was worried."

"I've been sick. Really sick. I'm fine. Just weak and tired and just finally getting better. So they tell me."

He looked down and then back up at me. "Can I get you anything?"

"No. I'm fine."

"Can I come in for a minute?"

I was afraid of that. But the cold air and the bright sunlight were killing me. It was a mighty effort to suppress a sigh, but somehow I managed it. "Yeah, if you get in here and shut that fucking door."

He came in and shut that fucking door.

That's when I saw his halo.

~

I backpedaled, gaping at him. He gave me an odd look. Obviously.

"You okay?"

I stared. I rubbed my eyes. Some part of me truly hoped it was my eyes. There was too much sunlight from outside. Maybe I was just having a moment. Maybe I was dreaming.

I pinched my thigh. Hard.

The halo remained. A scuzzy ashtray full of water after a storm, a bucket of water used to clean a very dirty house, rainwater on busted asphalt. His halo.

Another pinch and all it did was serve to piss me off.

"I need a drink," I said.

He laughed but followed me to the kitchen.

Given the hour, I think he assumed I meant tea or coffee, or maybe juice.

I found a bottle of whiskey in the overhead cabinet and poured out two fingers. Then I downed it.

"Lolly!"

He grabbed for my wrist and I jerked back.

"Don't touch me."

"What is wrong with you?" he said.

"Too much to explain."

Another two fingers and when I was done, I scoped out the kitchen. Weapon of convenience. Any contestants?

Of course.

He put his hand on me again, slower this time. "Tell me what's going o—"

I turned quickly with the cast iron pan. It was a 10-inch. The size I used to make my breakfast and the size I could wield with ease. And yet, it still carried a wallop.

I clocked him on the side of the head, and oddly, like the cartoons, that *bong!* sound is very accurate.

I had to laugh even as his knees buckled and he dropped onto my kitchen floor.

"Now what the fuck am I supposed to do with you?"

I sighed, made a cup of coffee, and considered the man who used to be my boyfriend.

16

MONKEY SEE, MONKEY DO. OR something like that. I'd seen it a million times in movies. Hell, we all have. Duct tape is your best friend while restraining someone.

Luckily, I had a roll.

I had him in a kitchen chair just as he started to stir. The chair didn't have arms. I wasn't that lucky. So I put his hands on his knees, wrapped a good length around his chest and the chair, then his ankles to the legs, then his hands to his knees. To make it strong, I looped the duct tape under his knees and up over his wrists and then did a criss-cross once or twice.

Fuck. I hope he didn't have to pee. But he was obviously a predator so let him piss himself.

I made a hot cup of tea, downed my antibiotic, almost coughed it out, so then took some codeine cough syrup. It was only when I felt that velvet slam of the codeine that I remembered the whiskey. Oh well.

The antiviral was done. I chucked it in the trash. I wondered if the halos would fade now? It would be interesting to find out.

I sounded like shit and looked like shit, but miraculously, was beginning to feel a little better. Not weak and unstable like a new-born deer.

I got tired of waiting for him to wake up so I filled a cup with cold water and tossed it in his face. Also as seen in the movies.

It worked. He gasped and sputtered to consciousness.

"Lolly?" He was confused at first. Then his brain caught up. "Lolly! What the fuck? What are you doing?"

"Who did you hurt?" I asked, hopping up onto the kitchen counter.

"What are you talking about?"

"You have a halo," I said, as if he'd know what that meant.

"What meds are you on? I think you're having a reaction. Let me . . ." He realized how very bound he was and suddenly paled. He started to thrash, which only served to hop the chair across the tile floor and rock it. When it truly threatened to tip over, he stilled.

"Let me out."

"Maybe. Once you answer me."

"What am I answering?"

I was so fucking thirsty. I just woke up. Why was I dealing with this shit?

I hopped down and got a big bottle of water out of the fridge. I guzzled a third of it and perched back up on the counter. A gargoyle looking down on the filth of humanity below.

"Who. You. Hurt." I enunciated each word as I stared at him.

"I have no idea what that means!"

I was losing my patience. I grabbed a fork from the silverware canister on my counter and threw it at him. It hit his cheek, tines first, and he yelped like a kicked dog. "Who did you hurt, Rich? Fucking answer me!"

"I guess . . . I mean, I guess in my life I've hurt lots of people."

I sighed. It felt like the air I exhaled had come from my toes. Like it was hollowing me out as it exited me.

"What child did you hurt? Diddle? Fuck? Molest? Pick any word."

He looked genuinely perplexed. So much so I squinted at him to see if I was seeing something that wasn't there. But no, there it was. His halo. Not as dark as the last one. But still very visible.

"I've never hurt a child. I've never molested a child. I don't know what you're talking about! Look, just let me out and I can—"

"Shut up," I said. "Let me think."

"—help. I think something is seriously wrong with you." He barreled on anyway. "You might be suffering some effects of—"

There he was, as always, mansplaining shit to me. It was part of why we didn't work. I wanted to choke him half the time.

This time I threw a butter knife at him. It hit him blade first in the forehead and he shrieked. It was way overdone for the actual event, but that was also Rich. A drama queen.

"I said shut up. Next time I'll dig out a steak knife."

His mouth snapped shut with an audible clack even as the stripe of pink flesh on his forehead darkened.

I stared at him. I stared at the floor. I stared at the bruises peppered across the backs of my hands, my wrists, my knuckles. Everything hurt because it had been a strenuous few days.

Then something clicked and I stared down at him, leaned my chin on my knuckles and struck a scholarly pose. I smiled. "Rich?"

He looked scared. More scared than he had so far.

"Yes?" He tried to act calm, but his voice quivered.

What was he hiding? What was he not telling me?

"Have you ever been with someone younger than you?"

"Well, you're younger than me!" He forced a weird little chuckle.

I hopped down, opened a kitchen drawer, found a steak knife and stood in front of him. "Answer the fucking question. You know I don't mean the two years between us. I mean *younger*."

His face shifted. That momentary flash of something reptilian. Ancient. Mean.

I leaned over and smiled. "I think you're not taking me seriously," I said, my mouth so close to his we could easily kiss without drawing any nearer.

Then I took the knife and drew a line down the back of his hand. I felt the resistance. The drag. The feel of a serrated blade biting into skin.

His eyes went wide and there was dead silence for a beat and then he threw his head back and howled.

I realized it was loud. Way too loud. So I hit him with a closed fist. His head snapped back even farther but he shut up.

I pushed a rag into his mouth so I could catch my breath. Then realized that was not going to work.

I snorted. "Silly Lolly. How can you confess your sins to me while your mouth is full of stinky dish rag?" I waved the knife point at his beautiful blue eye. Just a whisper away from touching it.

"If you fucking start that noise again, the next thing this knife gets a bite of is your pretty blue peeper. Got it?" I pulled the knife back a few inches.

He nodded so furiously I feared he'd give himself a concussion.

Pulling the rag out slowly, I got it free. Rich immediately gagged. I couldn't help but laugh.

"Jesus—"

"Tell me what I want to hear. You obviously know what it is. So just tell me. Or I have to hurt you. Badly. And a lot."

I leaned back against the counter, arms crossed, knife dripping blood onto my bare foot.

"Okay, but it's not what you're thinking."

"Uh-huh."

17

MAYBE IT WASN'T WHAT I was thinking. At least I thought that at first.

"She was my last girlfriend before I met you. I was your age."

"Twenty-one," I confirmed.

"Yes. Twenty-one. And we met at a big cookout thing my parents insisted I come to. We met, we got along, we went out walking and one thing led to another."

I wanted to roll my eyes, but I was trying to behave myself. "Go on."

"We ended up having sex in a barn that was on her parents' property. We spent the rest of the party talking and dancing and all that. I thought she was eighteen. She insinuated she was."

"Insinuated," I echoed.

"Yes."

"You know what they say about insinuating, Rich. It makes an ass out of you and me."

Then I laughed my ass off. He stared at me like I was crazy.

He didn't get my humor. Dumb ass.

Rich cleared his throat and said, "It was only when I was leaving the party that I found out she was . . ." He trailed off, staring at me with big, scared eyes.

Smart man.

I twirled the knife in the air in the hurry up gesture. "You found out she *wasssssss*?"

"Fourteen," he said.

"Fourteen!" I threw my head back and laughed. "Fourteen to your twenty-one."

He nodded. "Yes. See, not what you think."

"You don't think there's anything wrong with it?"

He shrugged the best he could. "Sixteen is the age of consent in Maryland."

"Say that again."

He looked at me warily.

"Say it!" I screamed.

"Sixteen is the age of consent in Maryland."

"And how old was she again?"

"Fourteen."

I drove the steak knife into his thigh as hard as I could. When his mouth unhinged and he started screaming I shoved the dirty rag back in there.

"You fuck."

He was still screaming like a lunatic. It was just muffled and snotty and gross.

"She was a child. If you were dumb enough to fuck someone without knowing how old they are, that's one thing. But once you find out," I said, leaning down so we were eye to eye. He was trying desperately to breathe. His nose was a river of snot. "You walk away. You just walk away!"

I pulled the knife out and that set him off all over again. The thrashing. The caterwauling. It pissed me off so I jammed it into the other leg.

"But not you. No, the great and wonderful Rich who's so amazing. Rules and social mores aren't for you. You're *special*. You just kept fucking her."

He was shaking his head vigorously, saying no, no, no with a mouthful of dirty rag.

"Yes! You said girlfriend. You mean to tell me you didn't fuck your girlfriend?"

He froze.

I pulled the knife out just a hair. Just enough to set his nerve endings on fire.

"Ah, see. Yes. Still fucking a little girl. A little fucking girl. You shit sucking dick."

His eyes went wider still.

I pulled the rag out. "Why did you break up? Tell me the truth now. Don't fucking lie. I'll know."

He stammered and stalled but when I made to ram the knife back into his leg he blurted, "Her parents found out!"

"They didn't know?"

He shook his head.

"Then she wasn't your girlfriend. She was your victim."

"No! It wasn't like that."

"No?"

"No."

"How was it?"

"It was . . . special."

"Yeah," I said, laughing. "Because it was illegal."

"I'm just a man."

I froze. Had he just said that? The theme song of predators, cheaters, and rapists. *I'm just a man . . . I was weak . . . I couldn't control myself . . .*

The laughter shook me so hard my legs felt weak. I couldn't stop. I laughed and laughed as he played background with mindless chatter of excuses and pleas.

When the laughter faded, I took the knife and plunged it into his neck. It slid in just above his Adam's apple. There was some resistance from his trachea but I prevailed.

It only took him a few minutes to bleed out.

I made myself a cup of tea.

I needed to think.

18

THERE IS A LOT OF blood in the human body.

I had an uncle who dressed deer when I was a kid. I couldn't go that far, I wasn't strong enough, but I found a painter's tarp in the linen closet and dragged him to the bathroom. I widened the cut along his throat and dumped his top half into the tub. I stood outside and held his long legs up as long as I could.

"This is bullshit," I said after about twenty minutes.

I was still weak. My arms shook, my head pounded.

I dumped the rest of him in the tub and went to see if I had a saw.

I cut him up as best as I could. It took a while. I used a small saw I had in the tool kit I'd built upon moving out on my own. I looked up all the "essentials" and got those. Some ancient man at the local small hardware store had helped me. He'd recommended this particular saw. Thanks, George.

I am pragmatic and a hard worker. I take being on top of things seriously. It's why I can afford a place of my own at my young age and it's why I could handle this.

I could totally handle this. It would be fine.

It was easiest to saw off the head and the arms. The legs were harder. I wasn't sure what to do with his torso, so I got a contractor bag and muscled it in there. Thankful it was winter, I dragged that part of him to my balcony and put it outside. I was on the fifth floor, so barring birds of prey, it should be safe for now.

I'm not proud of it, but I took a note from Jeffrey Dahmer and found my big stock pot and started the water boiling for his head. My father had started teaching me to cook when I was five. By the time he left, I could make dinner for the family if asked.

I had a lot of kitchen gadgets because I liked the latest and greatest. I usually played with it for a while and then added it to the collection.

I fired up the oven, found my instant pot, my crock pot, and my air fryer.

I stood back and surveyed the army of cooking implements.

"This could work," I said to the head on the counter.

The halo was gone but if I let my vision go lax, I could still see its afterglow.

I put the head in the pot and pretty much on autopilot added some salt, pepper, and a few bay leaves to the water.

I shrugged. "At least you'll smell good," I said to the face as it bobbed and floated along the surface.

I managed to break down the arms a bit more and put sections of one in the air fryer, some bits of one in the instant pot, and as much that was left as possible in the crock pot.

I stared at what remained and sighed. Into a contractor bag it went.

One leg broken down took up the whole oven rack. I lined the bottom of the oven with foil and hoped it would burn as it released its juices.

"Now what?"

I pretty much had everything set to slow cook. It would take a while. And then what? It would be easier to dispose of cooked, I guess? Less noticeable. Just someone throwing out old leftovers.

I snorted, took two pain relievers, and lay down on the sofa. I turned on the TV where a slick drama about demons and angels was playing.

I fell asleep fast. My mind and body exhausted from not only finding out about Rich but having to deal with him. I dreamed of demons and angels and greasy halos the color of cooking scum.

~

I was skimming the scum off the top of the stock pot when the doorbell rang. I froze.

Most of the bits of Rich had finished cooking and were just resting. They'd cooked and basted themselves (Rich was slightly pudgy) and smelled rather good. I had to keep reminding myself I wasn't dealing with some succulent pork butt roast, but pieces of my former boyfriend.

I tip-toed to the door as if the person on the other side could see me.

I peeked through the peephole expecting a cop or men in white uniforms from the local mental health facility.

Instead, I saw my mother.

"Lolly! Open up! It's me."

I straightened my hair and pajamas and realized it was futile. So I just opened the door.

She was beaming. "Hello, honey. Feeling better?"

She stepped in as I stepped back. My apartment was a cave compared to the brilliance of the outside.

She kissed my forehead, frowned, kissed it again. "Clammy."

"Still getting better," I said.

"It's today, you know," she blurted.

I searched my mental banks to try and figure out what she was talking about.

"Snow. Today. Today is the day she went missing and I was just at the psychic and she told me—" My mother sniffed. "Are you cooking?"

I couldn't lie. "Yeah. Just some stuff that was going to go bad if I didn't cook it. It might already have."

"Well, it smells divine," my mother said. "Your sister would be pleased."

She flitted into my apartment like a butterfly, her long swishy sweater floating around her jean clad legs. "The psychic said she is very happy, Snow. After ten years, she finally feels at peace. She feels vindicated."

I didn't believe in any of this but part of me warmed at the thought.

Maybe I had brought my sister some peace.

Come to think of it, I hadn't seen her today.

"That's good," I muttered.

My stomach rumbled and then my mother's followed suit. She laughed. "I didn't eat lunch and that smells so good. Any chance we could eat some?"

I cocked my head, considering the question. There was certainly *the chance,* but should we? Could we?

"Is it pork?" she asked,

I smiled. "Yes, it's swine."

My mother laughed again. "I'm glad you're feeling well enough to cook. You look like you've been through the wringer but an appetite is a good thing."

"I agree. Stay here. I'll be back."

I didn't have much in the way of something to serve it with, but I had some instant mashed potatoes. I doctored them with half and half and lots of butter until they were the consistency of whipped potatoes. The meat in the crock pot was fall apart tender, the meat in the air fryer a bit firmer and crisper.

I wiped a few hairs off the crisp pieces and laid chunks ,skin-side down, on the potatoes. I then portioned out some of the tender bits.

I laughed as I shook some dried parsley on top along with a little Old Bay. It would make it quite fancy.

We'd have lunch to remember Snow on her decade anniversary of being snatched. And what better way to dispose of a pig than to eat it?

A line from a song echoed in my head. *We slay the beast then we eat!*

Yes. It was time to eat.

My mother and I sat down and had a lovely lunch. She complimented me, her eyes on me the whole time as she talked about communing with Snow's spirit and finding some acceptance this year of all years.

She didn't know I had also been communing in my own way with Snow and that I had also managed to find some acceptance this year. Acceptance via action.

It was only when she went to get some seconds and I didn't stop her that it went south.

I heard her say, "Ooh, what's in the pot?"

I didn't say anything. I didn't move. I was suddenly very full and very tired.

Then the screaming started.

Eventually, the cops must have been called by a neighbor because they showed up, pounding, pounding, pounding until I let them in. My mother was still screaming. When they ran in to see why, they found out.

The Baltimore Banner
February 16, 2020

Local woman taken to state hospital for the criminally insane after feeding her former boyfriend to her mother. Lolly Valentine of Baltimore is speculated to have had a possible psychotic break after taking an antiviral for a bout of the flu. She is suspected in the killing of one local child molester and the disappearance of two others. She admitted to killing, dismembering, cooking, and eating her former boyfriend Richard Edmund Davidson of Perry Hall because of what she suspected was a former relationship with an underage girl. At this time, she is being held under observation and is denied release as the investigation continues.

19

I LIKE THE COLOR GRAY, so I liked my scrubs at the hospital. They were heather gray and very comfortable. No snaps, no zippers, no strings, of course. But they were very comfortable. So were the slippers.

I was still tired. They told me the antiviral could cause prolonged fatigue as could a severe case of the flu.

I slept a lot. I dreamed of Snow. She was always smiling now. And she was always glowing.

So, I'm pretty sure she's dead and that's good.

The thought of her chained in someone's basement all these years later is too much to ponder.

Someone asked me the other day if I'm regretful. I told them the truth.

"I'm regretful I didn't think of it sooner. I'm regretful I didn't have enough time and that I didn't get to more of them."

The woman nodded, made a notation, and left the interview shortly after.

Even in the mental institution, I had groupies. Patients who, in group settings, would verbally cheer me on.

Turns out nobody likes a pedophile.

At the end of my third day they brought in Doctor Kind. He shook my hand.

"Doctor Frederick Kind," he said. "I'm here to help you. I hope. I'd like to anyway."

I waited. I'd read once that if you were silent long enough it could prompt the other person to speak. Shrinks did it all the time. And since Doctor Kind was a shrink, I wanted to see if it would work on him.

It did.

"Well, let me tell you a little about me. I used to be a pediatric therapist but later decided my skills could be of much more benefit to young adults such as yourself. So, I came here about four years ago and I love my job. I love helping people. People like you, Lolly."

"I see."

"You look very young," he said. "Has anyone ever told you that?"

"Yes."

"Why did you do what you did?" He sat back, steepled his fingers like a TV shrink. It was a nice effort.

"I did what I did because I could see their halos," I said. I crossed my legs and started to swing the one on top wildly. Too much. Trying to control myself.

"Explain, please."

"I could see their halos of dirt and grime and sin. I could see it painted over their heads to show off what they'd done. Who they'd hurt. The innocent, the small . . . *children*."

He sighed. "I know it's hard. Go on."

"My sister was taken," I said.

He nodded sympathetically. An expression that always seemed to be on his face. "I know. Your mother told me. She is very concerned the anniversary was part of your break. That coupled with the drug."

I shook my head, picked at an almost indiscernible loose thread on my lovely gray pants. "No. Snow helped me. Snow supported me. And I was able to give her a little bit of closure, I think. All of us. I might not have gotten him, but I put a dent in their numbers. And maybe one day," I looked at Dr. Kind. "If I'm patient. Maybe I'll get him."

He stared at me, cleared his throat, regarded his notes. "There have been some interesting documented cases about psychotic breaks in people taking antivirals for the flu. Not a large amount, but enough to show some people may be particularly sensitive or have a severe adverse reaction."

"I don't consider that an adverse reaction. I think it was a gift. I think it was a moment of kismet. I think I did a service for my neighborhood, my town. And there are a lot of people who agree with me."

I looked at him, sitting there in his sweater and tie patting his balding pate and making notes, his writing so severe and staccato it almost looked like he suffered a tic.

"You really believe you could see their . . . deeds, Lolly? Now that you've been off the meds for a while and we have you on some new ones, you still believe you can see them?"

"I'd only know that if I ran across someone with one, right?" Now I picked a loose thread on my sock. They get upset if they see me picking loose pieces of myself. I tore a hole in one of my fingers the other day because of a bit of dry skin. I've been highly discouraged from doing that.

He sat back, smoothed his jacket over his lap, exhaled and gave me a big wide smile. "Of course. That's very true. So you don't see them anymore. You can't."

I looked up at Doctor Kind and licked my lips. "Really? Then tell me, Doctor. Why can I see yours?"

His jovial face blanched. He was whiter than white.

"Why exactly did you change your field of specialty? Why don't you work with little children anymore?"

I stood and Doctor Kind, he hit his panic button.

For Jason

Lady Vanity

1

IT WAS SITTING ON HER lap like a fucking pet. Her belly. Round and enormous and annoying as hell.

Frankie blew out a long breath and tried to inhale slowly. She was still peeing, so the urge to flee would have to wait.

What was it she was supposed to say? The belly roll, smothering her at the moment, was distracting.

"I do not always see my body as it is. I should ask others for their honest input. I should try on clothes instead of relying on my mirror and my mind. I should . . . stop fucking reciting this bullshit and go back on a diet."

She finally finished peeing and wiped herself. She stood and shuffled forward the three feet to the bathroom mirror. There, she severely bundled that annoying fat into a ball between her hands. When herded together with irate hands, it was a bit larger than a round of pumpernickel bread.

"And bread is part of how you got here," she said to the cow in the mirror.

Panic flared inside her, racing up and down her nerve endings like a brush fire.

"I can fix it," she told the woman in the mirror. "We can fix it. Eat better. We're eating for shit lately. Perimenopause has arrived," she said, shuddering slightly. "Bringing with it all its fat cell friends, hot flashes, sleep issues, and just motherfucking annoyance."

Frankie giggled uncertainly and took a deep breath. She sounded crazy even to herself, but it was hard not to let it out. That clawing anxiety.

The urge to unzip her skin and step out was almost overwhelming.

She hadn't been sleeping well for weeks. And when she did start to really sink down into some good unconsciousness, Alex's snoring woke her up.

More than one night, she'd entertained the thought of smothering him just so she could catch four or five hours of actual deep sleep.

Frankie gasped and realized her hands had become a vice around the offensive orb of fat. Her fingerprints were blanched into the dimply flesh. Anger ignited, joining the fear, and she gave it one final squeeze, as hard as she could. Didn't matter the pain she inflicted was on herself.

It was fine. It was good. She deserved it.

She heard the front door and Alex's daily merry greeting and let go of her stomach. She pulled up her jeans, buttoned them with a bit of a struggle and zipped them.

He'd know something was wrong. He'd want to talk. He'd get it out of her.

She regarded herself again. Her short blond hair, her big green eyes, the horrid pimple that had cropped up overnight on her chin.

"Stay strong. You're right. It's not your dysmorphia. It's your oldness."

~

"There's my beautiful wife," Alex called as she rushed into the kitchen.

Frankie snorted and moved toward the fridge, already trying to calculate what would satisfy a six-foot-six man's appetite *and* not add any weight to the boulder of fat around her middle.

He snagged her arm and tugged her back toward him. "Hey, woman. Where do you think you're going without a kiss?"

She stared into his big brown eyes and tried to steel herself. She opened her mouth, shut it again, opened it. But nothing came out.

Alex took the opportunity to plant a big kiss on her. He pulled her close, grabbed her ass and squeezed. She felt the bulge under his zipper and sighed mentally. He was horny. And normally that made her horny. But it was all so difficult with the weight of . . . well, her weight.

She didn't respond as she normally did and Alex, being Alex, noticed. He pulled back to look at her, taking her by the shoulders and studying her as if she were a fascinating specimen. She found that her eyes were starting to prick with impending tears and it infuriated her.

She chewed her tongue, wishing she could shove her hand into the waistband of her jeans and twist off a big plug of the fat growing there.

"What's wrong?"

"Nothing."

It was a pat answer and one that made him nuts.

"Frankie, tell me."

"It's fine. I'm having a . . . rough day. Just a rough day. It's fine."

Alex tugged her along by the wrist like a child. He sat at their funky retro table on a stainless-steel chair upholstered with red Naugahyde. They liked the retro thing.

He pulled her onto his lap and she locked her legs when she was almost seated. She couldn't put all her weight on him, she'd crush him.

So many women complained their men weren't observant. Frankie often wished Alex was less aware.

"What's this?" he asked.

She did her best to feign ignorance. "What?"

"This," he said, putting his hand on her thighs and pushing. He was strong. It didn't take much to push her so she settled fully on his lap with a thump.

She shrugged. Caught.

"Talk to me."

"I'm heavy," she said under her breath.

"You're what?"

"Heavy!" she blurted.

Alex laughed. It was a genuine laugh that infuriated her. "What's so fucking funny?" she snarled. Not like her. Not at all. She was usually amused and charmed by her husband, even after all these many years of marriage.

"You're not heavy," he said softly. "Look at me." He twined his fingers through hers and sat silently until she looked at him.

He stared at her. She grew impatient. Anxiety swirled through her center. The longer she sat on his lap, the more aware she became of her offensive stomach pressing against the very top of her thighs. The way her jeans strained against that roll. The way the button now dug into the spot just below her navel.

She couldn't switch to leggings, though. That was a recipe for disaster. She'd read it in more than one weight loss article. Leggings let you be comfortable. Leggings let you get fatter.

"I'm looking at you!" she snapped.

He took her face in his big hand. He gave her another kiss. It took everything in Frankie not to scream. It felt like she could feel the fat multiplying, growing, swelling as she sat there. This had been building. She'd been trying to do right and remember her self-talk, but there was no denying the report from her clothes: fat. And the information from the mirror: fat. And what the blob of flesh she'd held in her hands upstairs before he got home meant: fat.

"Frankie!"

"What?" She snapped back into herself only to realize he'd been talking to her.

"I said, this is your sickness talking. You know that. I know that. You need to remember how to deal with it and not let it spiral. You've always thought this of yourself and—"

She cut him off, her panic getting wild and ragged. She grabbed his grungy work tee. He smelled of metal and heat. "But it's not my sickness. It's menopause. It's weight gain. Belly weight gain. And I cannot. I cannot handle it. I've been so good. I work so hard. I just can't—"

She broke off in a sob and that just pissed her off.

He stroked her hair and let her cry. They'd been together long enough for him to know his words would be lost on her right now.

Finally, when she caught her breath, "Frankie?"

"Yes?"

"What if it is menopause? Then what? You might have to start from here."

"What does that mean?" It took her breath away, what he was saying.

"Then this might be an uphill battle and you might need to accept this is you now. I mean, I don't see anything different about

78

you—"

"Lie," she said softly.

"Not a lie. I don't. But if you do, it could be real this time. I know you've had other symptoms. But this is a normal part of life. Like gaining weight during pregnancy."

There was a sadness in his voice when he said that part and it broke her heart. Frankie had refused to have children. They had agreed—after lengthy discussions—that the weight gain would be too much for her psyche.

She'd never regretted it, but she always thought Alex did. And that it was the one thing he held against her in the secret part of himself.

"But I don't want it." It should be as simple as that, shouldn't it? I don't want it, it should go away.

"Well, I don't want the beginnings of this beer belly even though I hardly ever drink beer. Or these silver streaks up the sides of my head and in my beard. Or the fact that my dick sometimes takes longer to wake up." He pulled her against his big body and hugged her. "But it's part of growing older."

"I can't," she said. Her breath came fast and hard. "I eat right, I run, I work out, I get over 12,000 steps a day, and yet, when I sit down to pee, I have this thing on my lap."

He looked startled, raised an eyebrow. "What thing?"

"This!" she gasped, pushing down her jeans, grabbing her belly, squeezing it as if she could rip it off and throw it away.

She could picture it under there—yellow, bumpy globs of fat. Just beneath her skin. Which, while we were at it, wasn't as smooth, soft, or supple as it once had been. If there was going to be so much fat, shouldn't she be . . . buttery? Soft?

Alex gently pushed her hand down and said, "Easy, love. You're going to hurt yourself."

"I don't care," she growled.

"I do." He gently uncurled her fingers from her belly and winced. "You're bruising yourself."

"It's fine."

A flash of anger crossed his face and he said, "It's not. Now stop it."

She put her fingers in her lap. It only lasted a second. She had to tuck her stomach back into her jeans. It being exposed to the air— to Alex just acknowledging its existence—was unbearable. It made her face hot and her heartbeat too fast.

"I can't do it," she whispered.

"What do you want to do about it, then?"

"Plastic surgery?" The question slipped out, born of desperation and hope.

He sighed. "You know that's not possible. We're barely making it as it is. And I won't feed your illness. You are not obese. Your stomach is nothing but normal. I won't have someone carving you up because of your fear and dysmorphia. We have to work on this together."

She pressed her lips together, knowing he was right. About the money, that was. Not the rest of it. She'd have to find another way.

"Come on. Let's make an appointment for you with Doctor Bradley and then go get some dinner."

"Go out?"

"Yeah, why not. Splurge. Just for a night."

That made some of her anxiety recede. He could get a burger and fries—enough to satisfy his hunger. She could get a salad and pick at it. The illusion of eating without the actual calories.

"Okay. I'll put my shoes on."

They went to the corner diner. A hole in the wall with the best food and best service. They were simple people.

2

MOVING LETTUCE AND DICING CHICKEN into smaller and smaller pieces soothed her. The two glasses of wine helped too. She'd rather drink her dinner than eat it anyway.

They walked home, hand in hand, and she tried her self-soothing talk and tools.

Alex joked with her, kissed her hand, and when they arrived home, he shut the front door, tugged her close and kissed the side of her neck. A shiver passed through her and her nipples grew hard. The kiss turned to a bite and his teeth skimmed along her skin, raising goosebumps in their wake.

He still wanted to fuck.

The wine had made her warm and pliable. The lack of food had let it linger. She dropped her takeout box on the hardwood floor.

Alex moved as if to retrieve it and she growled, "Leave it."

She didn't want to lose the moment. The warm syrupy moment of peace. Because her clamoring, crawling unease would be back soon enough. She was in a loop. She was having an "episode." She knew how this went.

They didn't make it upstairs. He yanked her jeans off and then her panties right there in the living room.

Her mind chattered, *What about your belly?yourbelly?thatbelly?bigbelly?*

She shut her eyes and imagined the word STOP in big red letters. So big and so red they dominated all the darkness behind her eyelids.

He stuck his fingers inside her and her brain stopped for a moment. Everything was focused on her nerve endings and pleasure. He curled them, moved them, and whispered, "You're very wet."

Frankie nodded. She was.

When he moved her to the sofa she went easily. When he went down on her, she didn't look down at him. Which was something she normally liked to do. She couldn't risk seeing that extra flesh in the way.

He made her come and that lovely warmth tangled with the wine-soaked existing warmth and she rode that perfect wave of endorphins as he moved over her and then into her.

Frankie raised her legs to get him deeper and felt the extra bit of her press against his belly. She sucked her gut in as much as she could and that helped her ignore it.

She was close. So fucking close again. He kissed her roughly, holding her hands above her head, his chest crushed to her breasts.

"Roll over," he said. "It always gets you off."

It did. It always got her off. When he took her from behind he hit everything so well. And she could stroke herself as he fucked her. It made a good thing better.

But now, as he turned her, she wondered, was it because he didn't want to look at her? Didn't want to see his bloated wife with her distended stomach?

The STOP in her mind was not big enough to blot out that fear. When he grabbed hold of her hips and entered her, the fear of him feeling that doughy softness around her middle made her pleasure stutter.

She engaged her core again, shoved a pillow beneath her, anything to hide her flaws.

It was only because she was so far gone that she managed to come at all. He came a second later, not noticing her despair. They had eaten, they had fucked, they were still in love. Life was good. For Alex.

She was in the shower when he pulled the curtain back and said, "Doc Bradley's office called. He's away for a few weeks. Death in the family. You can see someone else."

"No. I don't want to."

Alex put on his stern face. "You have to do something. You're scaring me. How quickly you focused on it." He reached out to run his fingers over her belly. Over the bluish bruises there, no doubt. Couldn't hide those.

She pulled back. Not wanting him to touch her there.

"I can wait."

"No," he said.

"What do you propose, then?"

"How about Pastor Mike?"

She almost rolled her eyes but caught herself. Frankie was as far from religious as a person could get. She wanted to know, if there was a God, why was he such a dick? Why were so many people miserable, poor, sick, mentally ill, killers, rapists, child molesters? The list went on.

But Alex, sweet Alex, was a part-time Christian with good intentions who usually only asked her to go on holidays.

He was worried. And in all honesty, he had a reason to be. Pastor Mike would be as effective as calling a phone psychic, but it would make him feel better.

"Okay," she said. "Fine."

"Really?"

"Yeah, make the call if you think it will help."

He looked so happy, so relieved, she almost laughed.

He went off to make the call and she grabbed the wad of her belly and twisted. The pain ran through her abdomen like an electric current. She pictured it clearly, pulling and pulling and pulling until it all tore away. She could throw it away, or burn it (boy, that would stink), or feed it to the neighbors' dogs.

She heard the rumble and pause of his voice as he talked to Pastor Mike in the next room.

She finally let go of herself when her pulse pounded stronger in that flesh than in her chest.

She could hear him coming. If he caught her, he might do something more upsetting than making her see a pastor. He might take her to the hospital.

That had only happened once, and she didn't want that to happen again. She was so much better now.

3

PASTOR MIKE HAD A VOICE that could put anyone to sleep. When he spoke, it was more like listening to the murmuring of a distant television than a person actively talking to you.

Frankie's stomach ached from so much pulling, tugging, and pinching. Inflicting self-punishment for her failure to keep her figure only relieved her anxiety for a few minutes. So her stomach was mottled with blue and black and greenish bruises. It had only been a little over forty-eight hours since the fixation hit her hard and fast, and she'd done that much damage that quickly.

"—be assured that people love you as you are. A lot of this is your perception." He looked at her expectantly.

She was too fucking tired to ask him to back track to what she'd missed so she just nodded. The gist, she thought, was that Alex loved her as she was. She wanted to respond with "duh" but knew that would be rude.

He'd loved her since he met Francine Mary Louise Meyers when she was eighteen years old and convinced she was a fat piece of shit. In reality, Francine had weighed a whopping one hundred and thirty pounds and stood five foot ten. She hated her name, hated her body, hated her mind, her hair, her voice, and above all else, her belly and her ankles.

He'd loved her immediately. He'd been the one to nickname her Frankie and it had stuck. The name had given her permission to try a new life. A new thought process. She'd been able to make Frankie thin and pretty. And eventually, at twenty, he'd convinced her to see someone to help her. Help her make her mind and body try to sync up.

"—clothes?"

She'd zoned out again. Damn.

"I'm sorry. My mind wandered for a minute. What was that?"

But that's because your voice is droning and could put a lifelong insomniac to sleep.

"I said, have you considered being nice to yourself? Maybe a haircut or a manicure or splurge on some new clothes?"

She snorted. She hadn't meant to. Her fingers crept to her stomach, sore and beaten. She poked it once but when she saw his curious glance, she put her hands under her legs.

"We don't exactly have a lot of money. I wouldn't be able to do any of those things."

He leaned forward conspiratorially and said, "I'll tell you a little secret. I love to go thrifting. Thrift shops are what I do when I'm not here or doing church-related things. I love to find old things and make them new, or even find stuff I can fix and sell. I have an eBay account."

Pastor Mike said it as if he were admitting to having a VIP card to the local tittie bar. Frankie swallowed a laugh.

"They have some good prices. Maybe try there for some new clothes."

"I don't want bigger clothes," she said.

"Think of it as getting newer, more comfortable clothes." He steepled his fingers like stereotypical movie clergy, and said, "Those of us on the outside don't really see a change in you. But if you feel it, maybe something as simple as some new clothes, not even bigger, just new—to you, at least—could help your mindset."

She shrugged again. It couldn't fucking hurt.

She amended that to "It couldn't hurt" when she said it aloud. When he finally ran out of things to drone on about, she thanked him for his time, promised to keep him posted, and hightailed it, lest he start talking again.

At the first red light, she got a text from Alex asking how it went.

[Went fine. He suggested new clothes. Driving. Love you.]

It only took a few seconds for Alex to text back.

[Don't go too crazy! Money's tight. Love you too.]

She shook her head. "That's what I thought."

The thrift store was surprisingly busy for the middle of the day. She didn't have a shift at the convenience store that day, so she had time before Alex got home from the plant.

She wandered in, sniffing. The smell of dust and incense hit her and she coughed. An old woman with a red wig looked up. Her wig slid to one side and her glasses were cocked to the other. Frankie had to suppress the urge to fix both.

She kept walking, avoiding the curious gaze. The woman had a shopping cart full of oddities. A blender, three paperback romances, an old wooden statue of a bull, and one of those magnifying sheets they make for old people and the seeing impaired. She turned and stroked a disturbing baby doll and went about ignoring Frankie, which was just fine with her.

Frankie stood and took in the enormous store. She finally spotted the endcap sign that said WOMEN'S PANTS. She'd start there.

She found a bunch of jeans from stores where she'd normally shop and some from a few she couldn't afford. She took her normal size into the dressing room and realized her mistake. She should have gone up.

She stood there in her panties and socks. Her "new" jeans on the hook behind her. She was here. Might as well try them on.

The first two pairs fit fine until it was time to button them. Her eyes prickled and she took a deep breath. She would not cry. Not. Cry.

She took them off and moved to the other two pairs. One wouldn't come all the way up her thighs and the other wouldn't come up over her ass.

She looked at herself in the mirror. "Disgusting," she said.

She put her own jeans back on and felt the familiar bite of the button against her stomach. She put the jeans that didn't fit on the rack outside the door and went back to the pants section. She found a few pairs of jeans a size up and held them. She stared at them way too long. She wanted to set them on fire. She wanted to set the store on fire. She wanted to fucking set herself on fire.

She shoved them back onto the rack, muttering, "Fuck it." The woman across the aisle gave her a dirty look. Frankie stared her in the eye and said, "And fuck you, too."

She stomped off. She only realized she was holding her gut in her hands and squeezing it maniacally through her jeans when some woman gave her an odd look. The pain she inflicted on herself somehow soothed her.

She wandered down an aisle full of fake flowers and baskets. Then she hit the tacky vases and gardening pots. She took a swipe through the book section before moving on to records. Finally, she somehow meandered her way into kitchen goods.

"I could use a bowl," she said under her breath. "Make a cake in the bowl. Eat the cake. Kill myself . . ."

Another woman looked up at her and cocked an eyebrow.

Note to self: Thrift stores were full of nosy old women. Even in the middle of the afternoon.

She looked at a few bowls, recognizing two as Pyrex. The price tags were ridiculous given the condition of the bowls. But that was because everyone and their mother were currently still gaga over vintage Pyrex.

She settled on a clear glass bowl that was the perfect size. Three bucks. Not bad.

She went down the next aisle full of pots and pans and other kitchen gadgetry. When she spotted it, she stopped. Pale green. A wall mount. Twin blades. A thick handle. A cord wound at the bottom like a snake.

She was drawn to it. She swore she heard it whispering. She touched it. It was so vintage it was nearly ridiculous. It would look great in their kitchen.

The price tag showed the dirt cheap price of $7.99.

Lady Vanity was scrawled across the top in fancy script. She saw a bit of paper peeking out from beneath the cord and she fished it out. They'd crisscrossed the electric knife with tape to keep all the components together and keep shoppers' fingers safe. The bit of paper almost got stuck but she dodged the tape at the last second.

The legend *Cutting can be fun . . .* bled across the paper in red script.

An idea flickered at the edge of her mind. Sickened her. Her stomach rolled, fluttered, but then her mind purred, *It could work . . .*

No. The knife was great for their retro kitchen. And even Alex couldn't be upset with a price tag below eight bucks. Plus, if it worked, my god, she could plead practicality.

She looked around for an outlet and found a sign that said *TESTING STATION*. Frankie made a beeline for it and, after peeling back the tape, quickly assembled the knife. She fit the outlet into the receptacle and plugged the other in the wall. She took a deep breath, heart pounding, tongue dry, like this was some kind of life-altering, important test—

Because it is.

—and hit the button. The blade came to life, sawing back and forth rapidly. A dusty smell and some heat came from the vent at the bottom. She watched the blade shimmer and dance. She listened to its song as it cut through nothing but air. She imagined it slicing through meat. Fat. Gristle.

She smiled, watched it for just a moment more, and then let go of the trigger and disassembled it. She put the tape back where it belonged and wandered through the rest of the store. Nothing else caught her eye. Nothing else spoke to her. No other objects wooed her.

The cashier rang her up. It should have been about eleven bucks for the bowl and the knife.

"Eight seventy-five," the bored, pink-haired cashier said. Then she sucked on her lip ring.

Frankie looked at her and then at the items. "But . . ."

"Oh," the girl said in a monotone. "It's big savings day. The whole store is 25% off."

Even better.

Frankie left with her plain, clear glass bowl and her beautiful new tool.

4

SHE TRIED TO FOCUS ON making dinner for Alex. It would be nice to have it ready when he got home. She decided BLTs would work because there was bacon in the freezer and she could plump her sandwich with a lot of L and T and very little B.

She found herself mesmerized with the bacon as she slid it out and laid the pieces flat on a baking pan. It was easier to cook that way and less grease all over the kitchen.

Nothing like pork looked so very human in its rawness. She held a piece, knowing if she sliced a bit of her offending stomach off it would look very much like the strip of animal flesh she held.

It made her shiver in disgust and enthrallment simultaneously.

The knife sat on the butcher's block along with its mount and cord. The blades sat in the drying rack. She'd have Alex put the mount up after dinner.

She washed the lettuce leaves because she never believed them when they put PRE-WASHED on the label. Bullshit. No one washed that stuff. She sliced the tomato slowly, watching the knife sink into the flesh of it.

If she could just get plastic surgery or lipo, it would be fine. She did all the right things. Ate the right things, shunned the wrong ones. She worked out almost every day and put her all into it. She tried to get enough sleep, enough water, and enough sex. She fucking took enough collagen pills to create an entire animal.

She threw the knife down on the cutting board and grabbed her gut. She squeezed and squeezed. She squeezed so hard her skin tingled like a waking limb that had been numb for a very long time.

Then she took a deep breath and considered the small knife near the tomato. She picked it up and rinsed it off, and then she popped the button on her jeans and tugged down her zipper.

She stared at her pale gut. So big. So gross.

"You're not going to do this, are you?"

She dug the tip of the knife into her skin.

Frankie yelped. Her skin felt both hot and cold. The very tip was the only thing that pierced her, so she pushed in a little more.

If only her stomach was simply full of gas or air. It'd be amazing if it all rushed out and she could watch the grossness deflate before her eyes. It would be such a relief. So exquisite.

She dug the knife in a little more and all that rushed out of her was a thin rivulet of blood.

She considered pushing deeper. No. That was a lie. She considered slicing.

Something inside her hissed: *With that little thing? Come on, now, sis, we all know what you want to use. And it's not that little Boy Scout knife.*

She was just about to give it a go—what the fuck, right?—when she heard his keys in the door and then Alex's booming voice.

"Something smells good, love. I'm home!"

She hurriedly tossed the knife in the sink and tugged up her jeans. She wadded up a paper towel and shoved it between her waistband and her bleeding skin. God knew her jeans were tight enough now to keep it secure until the bleeding stopped.

~

She nibbled away on her bacon and ate some of her sandwich with economical bites. The fat and meat coated her tongue—she always cooked it crisp.

No matter what Alex talked about, her mind kept going back to the thought. Slicing. A nice thick bacon-sized slice of Frankie that would mean less pressure in her jeans.

It made her nearly drool with want. That wonderful random thought.

". . . overtime coming up soon. Will that be a problem?"

She snapped back into herself and found she was holding the tail end of a piece of bacon, stroking it lovingly. Alex stared at her in anticipation. Of an answer? Questioning her current lunacy? She didn't know.

"What? A problem? No," she said, improvising.

"What are you doing?" He took the final bite of his sandwich and started in on his chips. She hadn't served herself any chips.

"Wiping the grease off," she lied.

"Oh."

He was used to those weird things. He'd spent many years with her and her peccadillos.

He inhaled his chips and then stood with his plate. "Are you done, babe?"

She nodded. She handed hers over and followed him into the kitchen. She caught sight of the blades in the drying rack and they seemed to sing to her.

They could help her get where she needed to be. If she was slow. If she was careful. If she did it step by step it could all—

"What's this beauty?" Alex boomed and she jumped. Frankie giggled, more from the rush of adrenaline than humor.

"Do you like it? I found it at the thrift store. "

His face grew concerned. "No clothes, then?"

She shook her head and lied once more. "Nothing I really liked so I let it go for now. I'll try a different store."

When there's less of me.

She left that part unsaid.

He held the Lady Vanity and turned it every which way. Then he went about picking up the blades—her beautiful blades—and assembling the whole thing the way she had.

"And it works?" He raised an eyebrow.

She nodded eagerly as Alex attached the cord and plugged it in. When he hit the trigger with his big thick finger, she couldn't tear her eyes away from the sawing motion. The blur of metal. The way it vibrated with the motion.

She had a brief and bizarre image of him laying her down on the table and carving away her albatross of a belly, piece by piece.

Her breath quickened, her lips parted, between her thighs she went slick. Just like that. In a blink. The very idea of being relieved of this burden had aroused her so thoroughly she took his hand and said, "Come with me."

He put the knife down and followed her. Perplexed, sure, but unwilling to question it.

5

IT HAD BEEN FAST AND frantic. Frankie was slick and swollen from her internal mental movie and Alex always got turned on when she initiated, so she didn't have time to worry about her fat roll as he fucked her.

She came with a growl and that set him off. Any time she was animalistic, he responded in kind.

They stood in the kitchen, him eating the rest of the bacon like a machine. Post-coital love machine, she thought and smothered a laugh. Frankie envied him his ability to eat. She watched each strip get slipped into his mouth, watched him chew, swallow, then start again. He talked about the beginnings of a paunch but it wasn't true. He was almost identical to when they'd met.

"Not hungry?" he said, polishing off the last piece.

"No," she lied. She poured a glass of wine. That would do her. Calm her nerves. Maybe halt the constant movie in her head of her slicing a thin piece of herself away.

She knew it should be a disturbing image. Should be as offensive as the sound of nails on a chalkboard. It most definitely should not be a siren song that lulled her and drew her in.

She watched Alex examine the wall mount and look around. Having it on the wall would make it that much harder to ignore. And yet, she couldn't wait for it to be up there.

"Over here, you think?" He held it against the olive-green wall near the built-in corner cabinet. It fit perfectly in that narrow bit of wall space.

"I think that's perfect."

"How much?" he finally asked her. She'd been waiting.

She smiled and said, "Guess."

"Well, it's vintage," he muttered. He searched for a pencil in the junk drawer, found one, and then held the mount back up, marking the place with a light pencil stroke. "It has all its pieces and it works."

And it will be a life changing purchase.

"Yes," she said. "All true."

"Fifteen?"

"Would fifteen upset you?"

He shrugged and went under the sink for his small tool kit. He found a drill and some screws. "Not really. Fifteen is reasonable. I just didn't want you going to the mall and blowing a few hundred bucks."

"Pastor Mike suggested the thrift store. I figured I'd give it a shot. But it wasn't fifteen. Want to try again?"

He grinned and in his best creepy car salesman voice said, "Would you believe the low, low price of nine ninety-nine?"

"Closer, but no."

He checked the drill and it hummed to life. Sounding not unfamiliar to her brand-new toy. "Tell me then, I give up."

"Seven ninety-nine," she said.

He nodded. "Awesome."

"But," she said, holding up a finger. "It was a sale day so . . ."

Alex played along, making a drum roll sound with his tongue.

"So, six bucks."

"Wowza!"

He kissed her forehead and for just a split second she forgot all about the fat and the fear and the claustrophobia of having a gut.

Then her finger found that pierced place on her belly, that had thankfully stopped bleeding, and poked. The pain flared and her need to be rid of it reignited.

She watched him hang the wall mount. Watched him put the

pieces in. Even watched him read the little leaflet included and chuckled when he read aloud, "Cutting can be fun!"

She didn't know if it would be fun, but it felt very necessary. And she had a feeling it was going to be addictive.

She imagined it when they went to bed. Lying there. In the dark. Alex snored and she plotted. She tried to convince herself she'd never do it. It was just a fantasy. A way to calm her nitpicking mind.

But she thought she just might.

Frankie was pretty sure what sealed the deal was when Alex rolled to his side in his sleep. He slung his arm around her and pulled her close.

Something that had always warmed her heart and made her feel loved. This time his hand came to settle on that ball of fat. No matter how she wiggled, his hand was there. Pressing. Resting. Caressing that most offensive part of her.

Hot tears spilled out of her eyes. The self-loathing wrapped around her, squeezing her like a python.

Eventually, she fell asleep. The first thought in her mind when she awoke was that it was Alex's long day and she'd be alone with Lady Vanity for a long time after her shift was through.

6

"CUTTING CAN BE FUN!"

"I'm sorry?" The old woman gave Frankie the stink eye.

Frankie had to keep from responding with a vigorously raised middle finger. "Sorry, singing."

She was, in fact, and had been since she started her shift at nine o'clock that morning. It was stuck in her mind, that little catch phrase.

The woman *hmph*ed and took her bag with her cupcakes and her dog food and left.

"Old cunt," Frankie said to herself. Then she laughed. She was very aware it had a slightly maniacal bend to it, that laugh. And she was also very aware of not giving a good shit.

"Cutting can be fun . . . cutting can be fun . . ." She sing-songed it as she held her belly in her hands. She was hidden by the counter. She'd unbuttoned her jeans because they were just too fucking goddamn tight.

She took a deep breath, tried to relax. It was okay. It didn't matter. Because soon enough she'd fix that problem and her jeans would fit just fine.

"You okay, Frankie?" Mr. Roberts yelled from the cooler.

"Fine!"

"You're not giving Mrs. Grayson a hard time, are you?"

No, that old dried-up bit of gristle was giving me *a hard time.*

"No. She was in a bad mood today, that's all."

"Okay, then. I'm going in the back to accept a delivery. I'll be right back."

"Don't forget I leave at two," she yelled.

"I know."

"I have to leave on time," she said harshly. He had a way of asking her to stick around for another twenty minutes, or an hour, or sometimes more. Not today. "I have a very important appointment," she said, to make her point.

"Yeah, yeah," he muttered.

But she had news for him, she was out the door at two o'clock sharp. She'd spend the next few hours psyching herself up. She went back to her mantra.

"Cutting can be fun! Cutting can be fun!"

~

She kept her promise to herself. The moment two o'clock rolled around she whipped her vest off and headed to the back.

"Oh, wait, Frankie, I was wondering—"

"Nope, can't," she said, holding up a hand.

She had warned him. This was very important to her and she wasn't going to be even a minute late.

Alex had speculated he'd be about two hours late working overtime. She had until about seven to herself.

She was nearly giddy as she climbed in the car. Her hands shook. She felt the same way she'd felt on the way to her wedding. Excited, scared, dizzy, and lightheaded. Her heart pounded. She shifted in her seat, thinking of what a relief it would be to move around in her clothes and not feel the constriction of them. Not to feel claustrophobic in her own skin.

When she parked the car, she took a deep breath and ran her hands through her hair. She stared down at herself. It looked even bigger. It looked like the pumpernickel round of fat had expanded. Doubled even.

Fear lanced through her. She let out a little cry and grabbed it. Her button bit into her skin. Her zipper scraped the bruised landscape of belly below. Even having underwear under her jeans was horrible. Just that extra layer of fabric—of *something*—was uncomfortable. It made her feel mad and hostile.

"It's okay. We're going to work on this. We're going to get it done. You and Lady Vanity. You can do this," she said. Her own little pep talk.

She liked that the knife had such a regal name. Liked its jaunty feminine flair and the retro starburst on the handle. She liked everything about it, including the potential it held for her and her own piece of mind.

Piece of something . . .

She shook her head to silence the hissing voice.

Frankie thought she could look some stuff up on the internet, but it might scare her into not acting. Not acting scared her more than anything.

She took the components of the knife down off the rack and slid the blades into the handle. They clicked in with a satisfying thunk. Even after all these years, the thing fit together well.

She fit the cord into the base and plugged it in. She hit the trigger and watched it jostle to life. She held it to keep it running for a while and then set it down.

She'd do her best. She was smart and she was determined. It would be fine.

She grabbed a big bottle of alcohol from the cabinet in the kitchen and took off her jeans. What a sweet relief it was to feel the absence of their smothering embrace. She kicked them into the corner.

"You should probably put something down," she muttered.

She went to the coat closet and rummaged around until she found the beach bag. Inside was a big red beach towel nearly as large as a throw rug. Perfect.

She laid that down in the middle of the kitchen floor.

Her hands shook as she dumped alcohol onto a paper towel and began to swab the bulbous bit of her belly. It was cool and sobering. She was really going to do this.

"Are you really going to do this?"

Yes.

She glanced at Lady Vanity. "Are we really going to do this?"

The starburst seemed to wink at her.

She smiled. Glee and eagerness hit her in equal measure and she suddenly felt the way she had when she was little and she opened her eyes to realize it was Christmas morning.

What an adventure this would be!

"Cutting can be fun!"

Cold alcohol dribbled into her panties and she winced. Those would stay on to act as a guide. When she pulled them down to just below her disgusting paunch she knew where not to cut.

"I should burn you guys, right?" She realized she was literally talking to the blades and that scared her. But only for a moment because the fear was replaced with a warm feeling of acceptance.

Lady Vanity wasn't judging her, calling her sick, or telling her she was fine. She looked fine. It was all in her head. Or worse—that it was real and she simply had to accept it.

No, Lady Vanity was on her side and willing to help her make things right. Just them together. Two girls against the world.

She stroked the serrated blades and then unhooked them. A quick dousing of alcohol and a pass under some blazing hot tap water. Frankie got a potholder and grabbed the very top of the blades where they fit into the base and turned on the burner. She held the blades in the intoxicating blue flame, moving it back and forth a few times. She watched the stainless steel darken and thought she'd have to fix that later.

When she cut the gas, she set the blades carefully on a clean paper towel to cool.

She dribbled more alcohol on her belly and hissed when it hit the puncture wound from the night before. Soon, the puncture would be gone. Carved away. Forgotten.

She slid the blades back into the base, positioned Lady Vanity over her belly flap, and took a deep breath. She started where the puncture was. Not too far to the sides of her stomach. Not near the hipbones. She'd seen that once on one of those botched plastic surgery shows. If you cut too far over—she wasn't *exactly* sure where, but it was in the hipbone vicinity—you could sever the blood flow to the belly. It would basically rot and die.

She just wanted a flat belly. Not a rotten one.

"Here we go," she said to Lady Vanity.

Then she pressed the serrated blades to her skin. It was harder than she'd thought. Probably the sawing motion. Her belly wasn't cooked meat, it was raw.

Pain, exquisite and blinding, hit her. She almost let go of the trigger, thinking she'd pass out. Fairy lights encroached on her vision as she watched the blades saw through her skin. She had to look—there was no looking away—she needed to keep the cut as even as possible. She didn't want to go too deep in some places and not deep enough in others. She was aiming for a piece of bacon. Blood welled up but not as much as she'd expected. The pain had morphed into a euphoric peace. She felt sharp-minded and in control, if not a little shaky.

The flap she'd carved away began to sag and she marveled at the shades of pink, white, and red. On first glance it truly did resemble a piece of raw bacon.

"Just a little," she muttered beneath the war cry of the sawing blades. "Just a little off so that my jeans fit better."

Her panties were wet with blood. Her knees shook like she'd just had a shock of adrenaline. Her vision was clear but occasional star-bursts of light would go off in the periphery.

Somehow, magically, she hit the end and the piece of her flopped off and fell between her feet. One slice of her imperfections successfully eradicated.

She looked down, feeling a little sick. It seemed like her feet and the meat from her belly were miles and miles away.

"I need to wrap that," she said to Lady Vanity before sitting her on the butcher's block. She should have thought this through better.

Not so much blood. Not as much as she'd expected. But still blood. I mean, you couldn't cut into a human without getting it any more than you could cut into a lemon without getting lemon juice, right?

She walked toward the downstairs powder room, taking care to mind the blood on her feet and the wavering walls. She put her hands on the door jambs as she went, slowing down when the world seemed to move too much.

Finally, she reached it. Frankie sat down hard on the toilet. Just to rest. Just for a minute. She caught her breath and opened the cabinet beneath the sink where Alex kept all his first aid crap for softball and mountain biking. She found a brand-new ACE bandage there and some antiseptic.

She squirted the antiseptic on her glistening wet stomach and promptly screamed.

The scream startled her and she dropped the bottle. Then she was laughing. Great whooping laughs, sucking air, trying to remain upright because she suddenly just wanted to lie down.

She opened the drawers and found a clean guest towel. She put it across her stomach. It immediately dotted with red blossoms of blood. But not too much.

"So, that's okay," she whispered.

She wrapped the bandage around her middle, binding the clean cloth to her skin. Just to stop the bleeding.

"Won't take long."

She sat there for a moment and then looked at her fitness tracker. She had about two hours until Alex got home. She needed to clean up.

That was her last thought as she leaned back against the wall and shut her eyes. Just for a minute.

~

She woke with a start. Someone's car alarm was going off outside.

She sat up and screamed. This time it did not turn to lunatic laughter.

She clutched her tender stomach and remembered it all. She looked down. Pleased to see, even with the binding, how much flatter her gut appeared.

"Good job," she said. Then she belly laughed.

Every spasm was excruciating. And wonderful.

She remembered the time and looked at her watch. She'd lost about forty-five minutes to her beauty nap.

You passed out, asshole.

She needed to clean up before Alex got home.

She threw the wrapper for the bandage away and tidied the bathroom. She tugged her tee on over the binding bandage. Every step brought pain but she liked it. The pain reminded her she was being proactive. Going for her goals. Not settling for anything less than what she wanted.

That's what you were supposed to do. Go after your goals.

She made her way slowly down the hallway toward the kitchen and took note of the bloody partial footprints. How had she been so messy?

She found the mess in the kitchen and started moving faster. Fear propelled her. What if Alex decided to come home early? What if he finished faster than he'd anticipated? What if he was hungry. What if—

"Stop!" she said to herself. "Just focus."

She filled the sink with hot soapy water. Whether it was the injury or the steam, a hot flash hit her and she whispered, "Fuck!"

Frankie slowly got down to her knees and got the cleaning wipes from under the sink. She made lazy swirls at first, smearing the blood more than anything. The hot flash, thankfully, passed and she found some energy. She kept wiping and wiping until the smell of the wipes filled her sinuses and the blood was gone. She rolled the beach towel up and tossed it down the basement steps. The chunk of flesh went in the trash with the used wipes. She put the blades in the hot soapy water and stood there panting. She was exhausted.

"Sugar," she said to herself. Wasn't that what they gave you when you donated blood? A nice glass of OJ and a cookie. She had both.

She stood there nibbling the shortbread cookie and sipping juice. She wanted to feel better but too many calories wasn't what she wanted.

Her hand kept straying to her bound belly and even though it was tender as all fuck, the feeling of flatness was exciting.

The juice and cookie finished, she lifted her tee and peeked. Blood specked the bandage. Not a lot. The guest towel had absorbed most of it.

She gasped as she began to unravel it. Probably a bad idea, but curiosity killed the fat middle-aged woman, right?

She let the bandage dangle, thought better of it, and draped it over her shoulder. She stared at the towel, tie-dyed with her own blood, before taking an edge and peeling it back. Pain, hot and sobering, overtook her. Probably a bad idea to stick the towel right to a freshly cut wound.

She hissed as she pulled it back. The fibers had bonded to raw, bleeding bits of skin and her blood had cemented the fabric in places.

She hung her head and shut her eyes. If she did if fast, it could be bad. If she did it slow, it could be worse.

"Fuck." She pulled quickly. It was all she could do.

Frankie put her head back and howled as the pain hit her. Her feet and face went numb. Her pulse pounded. She felt like her temples would burst and she'd hit the floor.

Her vision sparkled and she chewed her lower lip to help her focus. She tasted blood, but that was okay because her vision sharpened and she felt better.

She put a hand on the counter and supported herself.

She dropped the towel in the sink and hit it with cold water.

"What, do you think you can save it?" she mumbled.

She threw it out into the trash with one sopping wet flip of the towel. Her panties went in next. She walked slowly—oh, so fucking slowly—to the bathroom and hit the wound with antiseptic.

It nearly buckled her knees.

But when her vision cleared she studied the wound and was glad to see it was raw and open and a lot of pink and white and red could be seen, but it wasn't as bad as she'd feared.

"Good, good."

She found A&D ointment, in the house from Alex's long-ago tattoo, and smeared it on the wound. Then she shoved a fresh guest towel over it and stepped back to wrap the ACE bandage around her middle.

"Nice and flat." A wave of giddiness passed over her and she giggled.

She was a proactive woman. She was going to make the things she desired happen.

"Like one big fucking self-help billboard."

She scrubbed the blades with a brush and then used a steel wool pad to get the discoloration off. It wasn't that she didn't plan to use it again for the same purpose, but she didn't want Alex to ask her about the black marks on the blade.

She did a sweep of the kitchen and made sure everything was clean.

"Good, good, good." She put all the pieces in the wall mount and kissed the starburst on the handle. "We did good, Lady. Thank you for helping me. Thank you for being the only one to listen to me."

She went upstairs to lie down. She was tired but not as tired as she'd anticipated.

She lay on her back and peered down the length of her body. She wasn't imagining it. Her stomach was flatter. She was well on her way.

The success brought a rush of arousal. Alex had told her no. Pastor Mike had told her to buy new clothes. But she had bought Lady Vanity instead and was taking care of business.

She slid her hand very gently down her stomach and then lower. It had long ago dried but probably still smelled of alcohol.

She parted her outer lips with her fingers and stroked. She got lost in it. Not really heading toward the specific goal of orgasm, just feeling pleased with the first step toward the body she wanted.

She didn't hear the door. She didn't hear Alex call out to her. Nor his feet on the steps.

She only became aware of him when he touched her wrist.

She opened her eyes and smiled.

He looked like he wanted to ask a question. Probably about the bandage. But she licked her lips and said, "I'm so horny. I'm sorta turned on. Fuck me, baby."

And that was something you didn't have to ask twice.

7

THE ROOM HAD BEEN DIM and her tee had still been on. It had been as easy as pie. She'd simply rolled over and gently pushed a few pillows under her belly. There was less of it. She could feel it.

Oddly, the pressure felt good, not painful.

Alex's hands had been hurried and desperate on his belt buckle. Like a man who feared he was dreaming. He wasn't.

Then it was just a dance of the urgent and the ready. She was slick and swollen and her mind reeled from what she'd managed to accomplish with just will power and Lady Vanity.

It had been minutes—sweet, stolen, and pleasurable—and then done. He'd rolled to his side, spooning her.

"Wasn't expecting that," he said, pressing his mouth against the back of her neck.

Frankie shivered. Now the pressure was off her belly, it thumped in time with her heart. It felt tight and hot but being aware of it was a good thing, she thought. It let her know it was healing and that she'd made progress.

"Is this what you do when I'm not home?" he teased, squeezing her.

She winced. "No. It just sort of happened. I laid down for a minute and then I think maybe I was half asleep."

I was in a dream state because of what I did. What I'm doing . . .

He kissed her again. "I'm starving. Did you eat?"

"Nope."

"Want to order a pizza?"

"Sure." She'd pick off the toppings.

~

At four in the morning, her belly woke her up screaming. Not literally. She wasn't insane. It was pounding like a rotten tooth and the ache and pain of it woke her.

Frankie sat up, ran a hand through her hair. Her body was drenched in cool sweat. Could have been a hot flash she blissfully slept through for once, could be her body expressing displeasure for the insistent pain of where she'd cut.

"Jesus," she sighed.

Alex rolled, touched her arm with his big warm hand. She pulled away.

"You okay?"

"Fine, fine," she snapped. "I have to pee. Sorry. Go back to sleep."

She stood slowly. The edges of her wound ached and tugged like the whole thing was going to rip open and her guts were going to spill out.

She shuffled to the bathroom and hit the light. Her image sprang up in the mirror, disheveled and haunting. Her hair stood up in ten different directions. She looked pale, her skin sagging, a single poppy bloom of blood had seeped through her sleep shirt.

She opened the medicine cabinet and was grateful when her reflection disappeared.

"Where is it?"

Frankie pushed aside pill bottles—antacids, allergy tablets, acetaminophen, ibuprofen, cough syrup.

"Everything a well-rounded medicine cabinet should have."

She finally found it in the back behind a big bottle of mouthwash. A bottle of Vicodin from her gallbladder surgery. They were over a year expired, but she bet they still worked just fine.

She opened the bottle, dumped them in her palm, and counted. Twenty. The prescription had been for thirty. If she was careful, the twenty should get her through her self-improvement project.

She put a pill in her mouth, turned on the tap, dipped her head, and took some water into her mouth. She swallowed fast, but not before the bitter flavor coated the back of her tongue.

She stood and took a deep breath, leaving the cabinet open so she wouldn't have to look at herself.

She rucked up her nightshirt and checked her bandage. Just the one spot of blood.

She ran her hand along the elastic beige bandage, feeling the flatter terrain of her belly. She didn't miss that bacon slice of fat. And tomorrow she'd remove another. She was getting there.

Frankie dragged herself back to bed. She put the bottle of pills on the floor on her side of the bed so if she let her arm dangle she could feel it. She lay there awake until she felt the drifting sensation that came with pain pills, the drug taking the edge off the gnawing dull pain of her wound.

It would all be okay. Tomorrow, she'd move forward. She'd improve herself a little every day.

8

FRANKIE REALIZED HER MOUTH WAS sealed together like it had been glued. Cotton mouth from the pain pill.

She sat up with her alarm and had to bite back a scream. Alex turned to look at her questioningly.

"You okay?"

"Fine. Fine. My stomach hurts," she said. It wasn't a lie.

He grabbed his clothes and bent to kiss her. "Gotta get in the shower. I'm running late as it is. Will you be okay?"

"I think so. I might . . ."

Call in sick. Take step two.

She couldn't. That would be bad. They needed the money.

She forced the words out. Testing Alex's mindset. "I think I might call in. I'm sorry."

He kissed her head and headed toward the door. "Do what you gotta do, baby. You're not a pussy, so if you need to call in, call in."

Joy hit her and then so did guilt. But she'd get over it. The better she made herself, the better she'd be in life. Work, love, and everything else in between.

Happy wife, happy life.

She sat there, getting herself together. She'd wait for Alex to leave before peeking at her progress. The curiosity was killing her. She was so excited to see how much better she looked.

She took the stairs slowly, the pill bottle clutched in one hand, making sure to grasp the railing with the other. She was ready for another pain pill, that was for sure, but hadn't she read it could thin her blood? Make her bleed more? Something like that. Best to wait until after. That's when she'd need it most anyway.

Her gaze kept straying toward Lady Vanity while she poured hot water into the coffee press. She leaned back against the counter and studied it.

"Are you ready?" she whispered.

Can't wait . . .

Her fingers stroked the bandage looped around her middle. She winced but also relished the pain. It was a good and cleansing pain. Something she could hold on to. It indicated hope.

Alex's boots clomped down the steps.

She pressed the coffee and poured it out into her mug.

"Babe?" he called.

"In here." Yelling contracted her core. Cumbersome pain skittered across her mid-section.

"How you feeling?"

"I'm okay." She moved the wrong way and must have winced because he gave her a one-armed hug.

"Take the day. Get yourself together."

I say we take you apart.

She almost chuckled and told Lady Vanity to shut up, Alex was here. But he kissed her and she kept it to herself.

"I will. I love you."

I love you and I want to be the woman you fell in love with, she nearly said. This is not her. You didn't sign up for this monstrosity.

He ruffled her hair. "Behave yourself."

"Never."

It was their normal goodbye exchange and it felt good. The impulse to lift her nightshirt and say, *Look, I'm making it better,* overtook her and she actually reached for the hem.

"Gotta go! I'm so fucking late."

Alex's boss did not believe there was any earthly reason to be late. Ever.

"Bye," she said.

Then she turned to her coffee and sighed.

"Here we go." A scoop and a half of collagen powder, a touch of baking soda (to cut the acid), a bare minimum of sugar, and then half and half. Just enough.

Her morning concoction.

Sometimes, she wondered if she was held together by collagen supplements and the sports tape she was constantly using when she had muscle aches or pains.

There would be no workout today. She had to heal.

She sat down at the table, put Lady Vanity in front of her, and sipped from her first cup. They'd have coffee together and then get down to business.

~

The wrap lay at her feet, speckled with rust-colored blood. The towel had come off much easier this time thanks to the A&D. Swabbing the area with alcohol to clear the ointment hadn't been pleasant. She'd hissed and cussed and her vision had gone fuzzy for a moment.

Once she was done, she braced herself against the small bathroom sink and caught her breath. A fine film of cold sweat coated her upper lip and her forehead. She felt it slide an icy finger down between her shoulder blades too.

Once her equilibrium returned, she stood and gripped her lovely assistant.

Ready girl? Ready to be better?

It wasn't so much that her knife seemed to be talking to her now, it was the sultry whiskey and cigarette voice. She pictured some silent movie siren with a smoky gaze and hair falling across her face just so.

"I'm ready. I just need to clean it one more time."

She did that as quickly as she could.

Some spots were raw, resembling blisters peeled of their protective layer. Some were scabbed over. A few spots looked like the fat that marbled bacon or fatty steak cuts.

She poked one. No pain really. Pressure, more than anything. A tightness.

Her temples beat heavily with her pulse and she studied the edges.

Along the edges, it was puffy. Swollen. That was probably just from the trauma, but just to be safe she figured she'd move out beyond that area a bit and trim it away. Today, she'd be better. She'd had some experience now. It should be better.

You're procrastinating.

She picked up Lady Vanity and nodded. She was stalling. Pain was a deterrent. It was simply a fact.

She hit the trigger and the knife hummed to life.

Frankie pressed her finger to the edge of her wound, but then moved it out just a bit. She should start about there. Letting go of the trigger, she positioned the knife, took a deep breath and hit the trigger.

The knife jiggered to life and bit into her skin. Blood welled up and her skin trembled from the bite of the blades. The hand holding the knife tingled and tickled with the vibration. The skin beneath the knife screamed with outrage.

Frankie forced herself to breathe.

Her vision wavered, going wiggly and bright at the edges. She kept guiding the knife. Never mind the pain or the blood or the fact the knife seemed lodged.

She locked her legs and tensed her ass. She'd seen that on Doctor Phil once. They were teaching a woman how not to pass out at her wedding because that was her biggest fear.

It worked. Everything stabilized.

The exhaust from the knife smelled hot and dusty because the blades were working overtime. It was time to saw off her second Frankie steak.

She giggled. Then she sobbed.

Keep at it. It's fine. You're fine, girl. Be strong.

She nodded. "Yes," she said to Lady Vanity. "I know. It just hurts."

Beauty is pain. We know that. Women have known that forever.

Somehow, she found herself at the other end. She came back into herself and cut just beyond the puffy border on that end.

Blood ran in rivulets down her belly, over her pubis, down to her knees. She could feel it tickling as it dripped.

She went down to her knees and wasn't quite sure how she got there.

Shit.

She put a hand to her middle and it came away slick. She saw flashes of something when she looked down that reminded her of what her grandfather had called "silver skin" when he'd butcher a deer.

She giggled. She was no deer, but she was on her way to being a sexy beast.

Another giggle. Her hand slid on the bathroom tile and she almost went down on her face.

The slice of herself lay next to her in an untidy heap. Lady Vanity had stopped cutting the moment she'd let go of the trigger. Safety first, kids!

"Cutting can be fun!"

She snorted and managed to yank the bottom vanity drawer open with a shaking hand. She stuck a bloody hand in and grabbed whatever she came upon first.

A handful of white and yellow guest towels.

Better get them on there, sis.

"I am. I am."

Frankie shoved them against her middle and found the original ACE bandage. She began to wind it around her middle to stanch the blood flow and hold the towels down.

It was only when she was ready to put the clips on the binding that she realized she hadn't sanitized or glopped any ointment on before putting the towels down.

That seemed exhausting.

Frankie leaned against the small vanity beneath the sink and shut her eyes.

"I'll do it in a minute," she said. "Just give me a minute." She forced her eyes open, but then let them drift shut again.

I wouldn't do that. I'd take care of business.

"I know. I know. Just a minute."

Her head seemed to be buzzing. Her consciousness felt like it was hovering a few feet above her body on a tether.

She felt wet between the legs but not from arousal. The room smelled of copper and hot dust exhaust.

She just needed a minute. Just a minute . . .

~

The vomiting woke her.

"Fuck," she said.

She'd puked all over her own lap. That was bad.

Worse, the shower was all the goddamn motherfucking way upstairs.

"Whoa, language," she muttered.

She moved and her stomach heaved again. The pain was so overwhelming it took her breath away.

She looked at Lady Vanity. "I didn't think this through, Lady. The pain pills are in the kitchen. The shower is upstairs. Why did I do this down here?"

The knife lay there unresponsive.

"Fine. Be that way."

She got slowly to her knees and another wave of nausea struck. She dry heaved, spit on the rug, dry heaved again.

"This is very elegant," she growled.

It was like a fucking horror movie, her bloody hands clawing up the vanity and grabbing the lip of the sink. She pushed against the floor with her left hand, hauled herself up with her right.

Every motion stretched her tortured, ragged skin.

Her vision kept winking in and out. She gasped for air. And then let loose a scream like some wild lunatic just to give herself a release.

She stood over the sink, swaying, smelling of puke and blood. She stared at herself in the mirror. Paper white, sweating, remainders of yesterday's makeup smeared on her face.

"Glamorous."

It was a tough decision. Drag herself up to take a quick shower, de-puke herself, and properly dress the wound, or stagger to the kitchen for those pain pills.

The drugs won.

~

Her feet left pink footprints on the white bathmat. Her head wasn't quite connected. Her mind was in another realm altogether.

The two guest towels she had mashed to her blood-weeping middle were fused to her. There was no way in hell she was going to yank them away. She'd soak them first.

Frankie ran the water to searing hot like she liked it, then thought better of it. In her mind, all she could picture was her mother dropping raw ground beef into boiling water to make bland food for their sick dog. The ground beef turned from a lovely vibrant pink to a dull, sickish gray almost instantly.

Could she cook herself? Could her skin go from pink and ragged, and yes, raw, to a dead gray shade? She wasn't sure. And she didn't want to risk it.

She turned the water to cool and stepped inside slowly. One hand on the shower door, one hand on the wall. If she fell and broke her neck, she'd have a lot to explain later.

That made her laugh. The laughter was very disturbing. It made her skin rush with goosebumps.

The one good thing was that Lady Vanity's voice wasn't audible up here. She'd left her downstairs.

The pain pills were kicking in, putting a muffling blanket over her pain. The downside was that they were making her head spin.

She clung to the wall of the shower. It was slick, some pink mold showed. She really needed to clean soon.

"What? You can't imagine Alex getting a scrubber and maybe helping out a little bit?"

She heard her own growling complaint the same way one would hear a far-off radio.

She stood beneath the spray and let it wash over her. It washed the scum of cold sweat and vomit away, which made her feel fifty percent better almost instantly.

She washed her hair and her body around the wound. The guest towels were soaking wet, weighted down with water. She slowly pulled them away.

The cold, clean water on her raw skin was like being stung by a thousand wasps. And the wasps were shooting fire and radiation and cayenne pepper out of their asses.

She sobbed, moved to grab her middle, and caught herself just in time.

The water at her feet was pink.

The urge to vomit hit her again and she swallowed reflexively, over and over again, to keep her wits about her.

Then she bit her tongue. Hard. The world slammed into focus.

A quick scrub and shampoo and she climbed out. Frankie squirted antiseptic down her middle and watched black spots appear in her vision as it hit her freshly carved flesh. Then A&D, new towels, back to the ACE bandage.

She'd need to get a new one before all was said and done.

All she wanted in the world was to lie down for a bit and then clean up downstairs.

Her cell phone started to ring.

She expected it to be Alex. It wasn't. It was Mr. Roberts from the convenience store.

Probably another question like: Where did you put the rubber gloves?

114

"Yeah?" she said.

"Frankie, it's Josh. Sorry about this being last minute, but I need you to come in."

Her mind ticked off the murder scene downstairs, Lady's blades that needed to be soaked, the vomit. Everything.

"I can't Mr. Roberts. I told you I'm—"

"Look, I'm in a pinch. If you want your job, you need to come in for the next three hours. I know you called in sick, but it is what it is."

It is what it is.

How she fucking hated that saying.

"I'm just—"

"Be here or don't bother coming in again," Roberts said and hung up.

She watched a fresh rose of blood bloom through the bandage and sighed. "I'll have to figure it out."

9

SHE WASN'T QUICK ABOUT IT and worried Mr. Roberts would fire her anyway. She'd had to bundle all the bathroom debris—including Lady Vanity—into the rug, rolled it up, and shoved it in the cabinet under the powder room sink. If Alex went home for some reason, she could only hope the smell of vomit would have faded.

She drove slowly because her vision didn't seem to want to clear. Whether that was the double dose of pain pills she'd taken or the pain, she wasn't sure.

She sat there for a bit, car engine off, to collect herself and regain her strength. She finally managed to get up, with just a little scream, and shuffled into the shop. Pushing the door open was excruciating.

Mr. Roberts was behind the counter. He looked up. "Thank goodness you're—" he broke off and stood. Leaning on the counter, he stared at her. "You look like shit."

"I told you I was sick," she said.

She moved slowly and watched his growing concern. Good. Served him right. A girl couldn't take one day off for herself? A mental health break? A girl day to do some beauty regimens to make herself feel better?

"Again, I'm sorry, but Vida couldn't cover your shift and I absolutely have to run out. Cassie is pregnant."

She bit back her words. Really? You don't say. Your wife is pregnant? Shocking! It's not as if you've mentioned it every five minutes for the last eight months.

She giggled and he cocked his head like a stupid cocker spaniel.

"Are you okay?"

It was a good question. She put her hand to her head. She felt hot. But she also felt cold.

"Fine," she said. She just wanted him to shut up.

She pulled her vest on slowly and shuffled around to get behind the counter.

"She needs me to run her to the doctor. I have to go. No choice. She's too big to drive anymore. Anyway, I see that you actually are sick—"

"You're a real fucking detective."

He let it slide. His face flickered with managerial displeasure for a moment, but he must have chosen to pick his battles.

"I'll be back as soon as the appointment is over and I drop her off."

She nodded. "Got it."

"Maybe have a soda? On the house, of course. You look like you need some sugar. Or some food. Have you eaten?"

She thought about it. Her mind rifled through the day and she realized she had not. Just her doctored up coffee this morning with Lady Vanity.

"Not really."

"Well, just keep a record of whatever you eat and I'll ring it up when I get back. I'll give you my discount."

His discount was a whopping five percent above hers.

"Whatever."

He looked at his fitness tracker and winced. "I'll be back ASAP. Promise. And then you can hightail it home."

He was out the door like the white rabbit late for the tea party. She snorted. He did remind her of a rabbit. Twitchy and skittish.

She leaned against the counter. Her mind kept going to some distant, soft and soothing place. Time slid by, untracked. Too fast, too slow, just right? She had no fucking clue.

The bell over the door jingled, snapping her back into herself. She stood too quickly and everything on her hurt with the sudden tug of movement. When the meat of her stomach flexed from the motion, she bit her tongue to stifle a scream.

"Hi," she managed.

"Hello," the woman sang out.

She was tall and tan with short blonde hair. Her jeans were faded, her tee was black, and she walked quickly to the back of the shop.

Frankie's world wavered. She plugged her code into the cash register with trembling fingers. She realized she'd never gotten that soda.

Pain pills made her nauseous. A nice cold Coke sounded good about now.

The woman came up with a smile and the clickety clank of a wrist full of bracelets.

"Just the water?" Frankie asked, ringing up the oversized bottle of organic farm-raised grass-fed center-of-the-earth volcanic water.

"Yeah, that's it."

Frankie was supposed to try to sell her a snack or a lottery ticket or whatever, but not today. She was too tired.

The woman proceeded to pull out exact change and fork it over.

"Bag?" Frankie sighed.

"No, that's okay."

"Receipt?"

"No."

"Thank you, have a nice day," she said like an automaton.

Her head was throbbing. Her guts were too.

The woman took the bottle of water then froze. Her blue eyes—very blue, Frankie noted—went wide and she said, "Did you know you're bleeding?"

Frankie looked down. She was moving in slow motion. Her mind vomited up the memory of having her wisdom teeth pulled. How she'd felt like she was moving underwater. This was similar.

"Oh, that? I'll take care of that. Thanks."

The woman leaned in. "Has someone hurt you? Do you need help? Do you want me to call someone or something?"

Frankie shook her head. "Nah. I'll be fine. I just had some work done."

Then she was laughing. The laughter came in big whooping

waves and was utterly excruciating, and yet, she couldn't stop.

She tried but failed. She slung an arm over her belly and gave a strangled scream, but the laughter just kept rolling out of her.

The woman took her drink and hurried out. The bell over the door went *ding!* Somehow, that snapped Frankie back into reality.

She picked up her cell phone as her vision grayed out, sharpened, grayed out, sharpened again like an old tube TV with bad reception. She pulled up Google and typed: *"foods to eat after blood loss."*

While it was pulling up (the reception in the DashMart was painfully slow) she went to the soda fountain and made herself an enormous Coke with just a little ice.

The actual ice freezer where they kept bags of ice beckoned her and she walked over and opened the door. She stuck her head inside and stayed there until she felt clearer. Of course, the clearer her head, the clearer her pain.

She looked at her phone while still hovering in the doorway of the freezer. The first thing she pulled up laid out some obvious stuff. Red meat, chicken, liver, beans. Her vision swam, but she went on to read fish, tofu, iron fortified cereals and bread. She snorted when she got to orange juice and lemons to aid absorption.

"I'm in a fucking convenience store."

She glanced up at the camera, knowing for a fact it was still broken and just for show. The light beneath it still glowed red but that only indicated it was on. Not recording.

She went to the hot food and studied the burgers. They were the closest she was going to get to steak. She selected the one that looked the least like a hockey puck and put it in a container. She squirted some watery ketchup on it and regarded it.

"I'd rather eat my own discarded skin flap."

She stared off into space for a moment, the burger warming her hand through the thin cardboard container. It felt like she was holding a living thing.

Where *had* she put the skin flap?

Finally, Frankie shrugged. Most likely in there with the other stuff, bundled in the rug.

Her mind wasn't on point at the moment. She needed food. Even this food.

She shuffled to the cold cases and found an orange juice and a bean burrito.

She put the burrito in the microwave. She'd alternate bites of

burger and burrito, wash it down with Coke and OJ and then—
"Barf everywhere," she said. That crazy laugh was back and she let it go. Whatever. There was no one here to question her sanity. Just herself. And she declared herself just fucking fine.

The microwave dinged and she picked removed the burrito. It was blazing hot and caught her off guard. She juggled it a moment before chucking it overhand toward the counter. It landed on the tile with a splat, luckily still in its outer wrapper.

"And I was so fucking close," she said.

She shuffled toward the counter, feeling very much like an old lady. She could feel a tugging at her belly. The wound was probably seeping and then crusting over. Not very attractive but it was—

"Just temporary!" she sang out.

Her head went buzzy and light for a second and she considered sitting down right there in the aisle. But she managed to keep going and eventually—after six or seven years it felt like—she reached the counter. She dropped onto the stool they weren't supposed to use, but was kept there anyway, and stared at the gray-brown meat.

"Dinner is served."

10

THE BURGER WAS LIKE CHEWING an eraser, but the fucking burrito was the real nightmare. Frankie choked down as much as she could. She washed it down with fountain soda, saving the OJ for last.

She watched the front door like it was going to perform for her. It was the constant motion of traffic outside the thick glass that mesmerized her.

When the door was flung open and the bell jingled she jumped before managing a "Hello," which was second nature after all these years.

Three kids came through and she watched them head down the candy aisle. They were regulars and she knew pretty much what they'd bring up.

She faded back out into lala land until they were presenting her with three slushies, two candy bars, and a porn magazine.

She took it and slid it under the counter. "Nice try, guys."

Ricky, the smallest, shrugged. He lived in her neighborhood so she knew he was slight for his age. He looked like he was eleven but was about fourteen.

"We had to try," he said.

Frankie laughed and rang up the rest. The tallest forked over a twenty, no doubt his allowance, and paid for the whole thing.

"Big spender," she muttered.

"Birthday money," he said, correcting her.

"How old?" she asked.

Her head was ringing. It was like hearing far-off machinery. She felt like shit, but she also felt floaty and ethereal from the pain meds.

"Sixteen," he said, puffing up.

It was Frankie's turn to shrug. "Close enough," she said. She retrieved the magazine and pushed it across the counter. "You didn't get that from me."

They all nodded, eyes wide, laughing. They snatched the magazine and took off, practically running in case she changed her mind.

Then the door suddenly swung open again and the little one poked his head in. "You know you're bleeding?"

She nodded. "Yeah, I know," she said, bored with it.

When he left, she managed to launch herself off the stool and headed toward the first aid aisle. Next to overpriced vials of pain relievers and allergy pills was a small section of Band-Aids and two dusty knock-off ACE bandages. She took both.

Let Mr. Roberts fire her. Fuck him.

She flipped the sign to "Back in Ten Minutes." A sign they were only supposed to use for emergencies. Bleeding to death seemed like an emergency.

You're not bleeding to death . . .

Lady Vanity's voice in her head. How was she hearing her all the way out here at work?

Didn't matter.

She took the bandage knowing there was a bottle of alcohol and a tube of Neosporin in the dingy employee bathroom. She'd do her best.

The light in the bathroom made her feel like she was in a cell block movie from the seventies.

Her skin was slick with cold sweat and a wave of vertigo hit her. Perimenopause hormone related vertigo or cutting bits of oneself off vertigo, she wondered.

"Tomato, toe-mah-toe," she whispered.

She took off her vest and then her tee. It felt like it took forever.

Back in ten minutes her ass.

Her current bandage was spotted with rust-colored starbursts. The skin beneath not only ached, it burned. Every motion to unroll the elastic bandage set off a firework of pain.

She chewed her lower lip, tasted blood, and kept going.

When the bandage was off, she set it in the sink. She'd take it home in a bag and wash it. No use getting rid of any of them until her transformation was totally done.

She pulled the pads away from her belly. The meager light illuminated dried rivulets of blood, spots still seeping fresh blood. There were a few places the color of the eye rounds she made for dinner. Alex's favorite. And the sick, bumpy yellow pockets of pure fat. Those bothered her the most. But overall, she was pleased.

She turned to the side. Despite the puffing and a slight bit of blackening to one side (either very dark dried blood or possibly necrotic flesh, her brain whispered) she was satisfied with her progress.

Less poof in the belly area. Less paunch. Less punch in the gut *mass*. Less . . .

She shook her head and the long unwinding thought ceased.

"Right. Let's clean this. Tomorrow I can trim off that black bit and get some of that yellow shit. That disgusting, bumpy cottage cheese fat." It all came out in a hiss.

She unrolled a wad of toilet paper and doused it in alcohol. Ideally, she'd have a squirt bottle and just douse her front, but that wasn't doable. So, she dabbed at it daintily, wondering if Lady Vanity would be pleased with her work.

She used the whole bottle of alcohol, her mind in a fog. Then she used the rest of the Neosporin. It wasn't nearly enough.

She had no new towels so she flipped them over and laid them across the expansive wound. Blowing the dust off the bandage, she peeled the plastic away from the backing and went about mummifying herself.

Then a shuffle back out to the counter after burying the evidence in the trash.

She flipped the sign, sipped her soda, roosted on the stool and waited.

When Josh got back she was so out of here. She still had to go home and clean the house.

~

The pain pill got lodged in her throat and her mind snickered: *Carving yourself up like a Christmas ham and you're going to choke to death on expired Vicodin.*

It finally went down and she sucked in a breath. Then she coughed. The cough brought tears to her eyes and she just kept crying.

She hadn't anticipated the pain to be this bad. With every hour that passed, it got worse.

She shoved everything but Lady Vanity in a trash bag. Her face and neck and beneath her boobs were drenched with sweat. A fine tremor moved through her and she realized she was shivering. Her head and neck were hot but her skin was slick and cool.

It took her a long time to drag the very light trash bag out to the can. Equally as long to go back in and start the hot water to soak the blades.

Her hands were shaking. Her head was far away and her vision looked like a soap opera dream.

You know, you could go try on your jeans while these soak. See how much better you're doing. I bet just one more session together and we'll have you where you want to be.

Lady Vanity's sultry voice filled her head and she nodded as she dropped the blood and fat crusted serrated blades into hot soapy water.

Dusk was just starting to settle. She still had time before Alex came home. She thought. His schedule was up in the air, but it was probable.

"It's probably probable," she said in a sing-song. Then she answered Lady Vanity as an afterthought. "Okay, let's go try on my jeans."

The double down of Vicodin was putting a numbing blanket on her wounds.

She made sure to keep a hand on the wall as she walked. Her gait was a bit off, her belly and upper thighs sticky. Her mouth was super fucking dry. She should have gotten a drink before heading up the steps.

Too late, though, she was already there. Each step seemed ten feet high. Every time she lifted her foot it was a struggle. She hauled herself up slowly but surely, keeping a death grip on the banister.

There were two steps into her bedroom from the main hallway. She was so exhausted she found them offensive. As if someone had put them there just now to slow her down.

She got into her room and dropped to the bed with a sigh. There was a bottle of barely touched spring water on her nightstand.

Frankie could have cried, she was so happy.

She twisted off the cap and sat there, sipping water, feeling the room moving ever so slowly like she was sitting in a small craft floating on water.

It was not an entirely unpleasant feeling.

You should move some. Let's try on those jeans.

"Yes, those jeans."

Frankie rose and went to the ottoman near the ugly pink chair standing vigil in the corner of the bedroom. Her jeans weren't there.

"Damn." She tottered to the closet and checked the small stack of clothing. Nope. Then she looked at the hangers where her jeans usually hung. Nope.

"Fuck."

That left the hamper. She made her way back across the room, a distance that felt very much like a marathon run, and flipped the lid up. There they were.

It was an effort to get them out and turn them right side out. She sat on the edge of the bed and fed her legs through each leg hole. She was panting by the time they were both in.

"Just a little rest," she whispered, sitting there, jeans around her thighs. She took note that there was less belly resting on the very tops of her thighs and that made her very happy.

Finally, curiosity won out and she stood precariously and drew the jeans up. They buttoned a bit easier. It wasn't her imagination. The button fed through the hole easily. The zipper drew up like a hot knife through butter. Was that the saying? She was pretty sure.

Without the bandage and the towels and that pesky swelling it's probably even flatter than you think . . . Lady Vanity's whisper was sultry in her ear.

"Yes," she said.

Yes, came the echo.

Frankie wanted to go on a spree and try on all the clothes in her closet. She wanted to see what fit better now that she was fighting menopause and weight gain on her terms. But she was too fucking tired.

She shucked the jeans and tossed them in the general direction of the hamper. Then she lay down on her side. "Just a few minutes," she said.

Just a little while to sleep. Not much. Just a little.

11

HIS HAND ON HER BELLY woke her. Hot and heavy. She winced and tried to toss it off. The TV was flickering its blue light at her and she squinted to try and read the alarm clock.

Eleven p.m.

Alex snored heartily next to her. The annoyance that slammed her was sudden. It made her fully alert, as did the pain. Heavy, dull, somehow oily. She'd been asleep much longer than she'd expected.

Alex mumbled something and she tried to move slowly so she wouldn't rouse him. But he caught her as she was about to sit up. He tugged her arm and that motion went straight to her wound. The sucking, tearing, ripping sensation that came with ragged open wounds made sweat break out on her upper lip.

"Hey. What's with the bandage? You okay?"

"I got called in and pulled my back," she said. Lying on the spot wasn't normally her forte but she knew if Alex even suspected she was doing some self-improvement work he'd lose his mind.

He worried too much. He always had.

"Need anything?"

"Just to pee," she said, getting herself upright and swinging her legs around to get her feet on the floor. It was an awkward and rusty move. A marionette whose strings had been partially cut.

"I got home about an hour ago," he mumbled. "Tried to watch TV. Failed . . ." Then he was back to snoring.

She smiled. She loved him even if he sounded like a woodchipper devouring a tree.

It was a lot of work to get herself downstairs to the pain pills in the kitchen. She stood at the fridge, door cracked open, air cooling her hot, damp skin. She swallowed two pills with some orange juice.

She should eat something, but the thought of doing so made her stomach flip sickly.

Just juice.

She scrubbed the blades next, watching small flecks of herself disappear down into the drain. Red, white, yellow like chicken fat, gray. All the colors of her. All the parts of her that were unwanted and unnecessary.

"Good riddance."

She tucked the Vicodin under her arm and went back upstairs realizing she was just in a tee and panties. Her jeans were upstairs and so were her work pants.

She crawled back into bed and pulled just the sheet over herself. It felt like a hot flash kind of night.

The TV continued to flicker. No doubt Alex had set the sleep timer. He always did.

She let the silvery blue light lull her to sleep.

Just as she was drifting back to sleep on a drugged wave, she heard Lady Vanity whisper, *One more will probably do. We'll have to go a bit deeper this time, but that's okay.*

"That's okay," she answered.

~

Her eyes flew open when Alex kissed her on the forehead.

"You're clammy," he said. "Still not feeling well or hot flash?" He gave her a wry smile. More than once he'd pulled her close to cuddle in the morning and there it had come, a searing claustrophobic heat that would have her kicking off the covers so she could breathe.

Her stomach rolled sickly. Her body ached. The skin of her belly beneath her makeshift bandages felt both too taut and too loose.

"Not sure," she said.

"Do you work today?"

She shook her head. Bad move. The world shimmied around, showing no signs of stilling.

She blinked hard and bit her tongue. That helped sharpen things.

Alex brushed her damp hair back and said, "You should stay home if you can."

"That's the plan," she said.

"You look pale."

"I'm fine. You worry too much."

"Can't help it, babe. I love you."

"I love you too," she said. "Go to work. I'm fine. I'll go down and make some tea and find some food."

"Want me to bring you some?"

She considered it but thought better of it. She had to get up. There were things to do. She couldn't lounge in bed all day. She was so close.

"Nah. Go on. Get." She offered him a smile and he left.

She swayed when she stood and barely managed to make it to the bathroom before she puked her guts up.

Pain pills without food often fucked with her. That had to be it.

Her reflection showed pasty skin, sweat matted hair, and dark circles beneath her eyes. She'd looked better, that was for sure.

She put on very loose pajama pants that hung low on her hips and shoved the pill bottle in her pocket. Frankie made her way downstairs at a snail's pace. But fuck it, it wasn't a race, was it? She found a bottle of soda and swallowed two pills before thinking about it.

"Shit. Probably shouldn't have taken those *first*."

So be it. She wouldn't let it stop her.

She set the blades in a shallow aluminum pan and poured the rest of the rubbing alcohol over them. She'd need to be very careful since she was going deeper today.

We got this, Lady Vanity said. Frankie smiled at the wall attachment. Her fingers caressed the retro starburst on the trigger. They were almost there.

"Almost there," she whispered to Lady Vanity. Then as a battle cry to get herself psyched she said, "Cutting can be fun!"

Yes, cutting can be fun.

This was exactly what she needed. She would not go silent into that good night. She would kick and scream the whole way. She'd fight every atrocity, every indignity as long as humanly possible.

When everything was ready, she stood there. Should she haul all this shit upstairs near the shower, or keep it all down here near the sink?

Her brain didn't want to come to a definitive decision. It kept swirling down pathways and labyrinths. Even veering off occasionally to try and remember the last thing she'd eaten.

She walked on numb legs to the small bathroom and turned on the light. It was stuffy in there and sweat rolled in freezing cold lines from her fat armpits.

Not fat.

Hot.

Hot, she thought.

She unwound the bandage slowly, put her trembling fingers on the tops of the towels and stopped. Some part of her, way deep down where the truth lived, screamed in terror at the thought of pulling the makeshift dressing away.

She took a deep breath, that didn't help at all, seeing as the room was still moving restlessly. Lady Vanity sat there on the sink edge, plugged in and ready to cut.

She pulled gingerly at first but then the mozzarella cheese happened. Frankie blinked. Mozzarella cheese? No, it wasn't.

She shook her head and reached up with her free hand and smacked herself in the face as hard as she could. Her ears rang and bright Christmas lights flashed in her vision before it finally cleared.

She looked down even though she didn't want to. She saw what she had anticipated: the raw hamburger pink, the mottled purplish-blue and the stuff that reminded her of silver skin, the mocking bulbous bits of fat. But there was that cheese like substance. And a smell. Like hot garbage sitting in the sun.

She touched the string that ran from cloth to belly. Rubbed it between her fingers.

It was pus. Infection. She recalled only one time like this in her life. When she'd cut her ankle pretty damn bad right over the bone and her mother had told her to not be such a baby.

She'd gone about her life, not doing much to it. After a softball game, it itched and stung and hurt. She'd pulled her tube sock down and long strings of infection had bound her sock to her wound.

This was the same but on a much bigger scale.

"Guess I'll have to trim that part away," she said. "It'll be fine. I'll do better."

Modifications can be tricky but we can do this . . .
Lady Vanity always made her feel so much better.

She shut her eyes and yanked the rest of the towels from her body. It ripped where it had fused to wounded flesh, and she whimpered like a dog who'd just been beaten. She felt wet heat coat her skin and knew parts of it were bleeding again.

Sometimes pulling off scabs could aid healing. She'd read that somewhere.

Despite the pus and the puffiness and more of that ugly black skin at the edge, she was looking pretty damn good. Her belly was much less intrusive than it had been just a few days before.

"You can do this. We can do this," she told her pasty reflection.

She took off all her clothes, because what was the point of leaving any on? Then she took a larger beach towel from under the sink and laid that on the floor.

She stood on it and regarded her belly. She couldn't see herself below the shoulders in the small mirror. She looked underneath the sink and found the peroxide bottle. She tipped it over her midsection and a little dribbled out. But not much. Not nearly enough.

"Oh, shit." She hadn't thought to check the supply. She knew there wasn't any upstairs or in the kitchen. This was it. She could get dressed and run out for more or she could improvise.

Frankie kept a death grip on the edge of the sink and looked underneath it. Way in the back was a spray bottle. She regarded it. *Kills 99.9% of germs.*

She'd read an article once upon a time that this and other household cleansers had been used to clean skin and so much more midcentury.

"Couldn't hurt."

Wrong. It hurt like fury. It burned like fire. Her eyes watered constantly and she gagged as she sprayed her wound until she could hardly breathe in the tiny half bath.

She stuck her head outside the door and gulped in clean air from the hallway.

She hit the overhead fan and waited a few minutes for the fumes to clear. She stepped back in and regarded her foaming, bubbly, antiseptic slicked skin.

There's really no point wiping all that excess pus off. You'll cut it away anyway, the knife said.

"Good point."

131

She fired it up, smelling the hot dust scent of its exhaust. She could feel the warm air of it on her skin as she cut the engine and then positioned the blades outside the existing wound. Just a little beyond what was there. Just a tad outside that perimeter.

Not too far out. That would be dangerous.

She stared at the blades. Was she really going to do this?

Of course you are. You're a bad ass bitch who will not go silently into that fat night . . .

"And cutting can be fun," she answered.

She hit the trigger and the blades jumped to life. It stalled, staggering against the tougher skin it was tackling today. She chewed her lower lip in concentration, glad the pain pills had kicked in. Glad she was brave. That she was a bad ass bitch. Glad she'd found Lady Vanity instead of some ugly fat pants for ugly, fat middle-aged women who worked so goddamned hard and it just wasn't fair.

"It's just not fair," she muttered, chewing her lip harder. She tasted blood. She wasn't sure if it was from her lip or from the blood splattering as she cut. She blinked some away and kept going, realizing it really didn't matter.

Her ears buzzed like phantom cicadas in high summer. Her vision swam. She gritted her teeth and just kept going.

Through the red meat (good for iron after blood loss!) and horrid yellow fat and the purply silver bits too.

Blood poured down her crotch, her upper thighs, her knees. It dripped around her feet, hot and slick, but she just kept going because honestly, fuck it.

Fuck. It.

Her jeans would fit better and hot flashes and acne and night sweats and achy joints and vertigo would all be so much easier to handle if her pants just simply fucking fit properly.

Because she worked so hard and it just wasn't fair.

Not fair.

No, it isn't.

Lady Vanity whispered to her as her knees buckled and she hit the floor. She heard the buzzing of the knife stop when she dropped the base.

She felt so much lighter. She felt so much better. Her stomach was flatter. She pushed her hand to it and it came away hot and slick.

She wanted to see, but her vision had been eaten by a giant black circle and the room smelled like wet pennies.

~

You should probably move . . .

She woke to the whispers. Her hand still rested in the warm, soupy wetness. It took her a second to remember what it was. It was her. Her stomach.

She felt around and screamed at the pain. She hissed air in and out like a woman giving birth. *Lamaze to give birth to the new you!* her mad brain screamed.

It took her a fucking excruciating year to sit up and when she looked down she gagged. She was a sheet of red from modified belly to feet. It was still seeping.

"This isn't good. This isn't stopping," she mumbled. Her tongue felt too big, her mind too small. The room was moving and she steadied herself with a hand on the floor.

Stopping the bleeding was key. Binding it wouldn't do. She'd have to do more than that.

Cauterize it.

She nodded. Good thinking, Lady Vanity. She crawled toward the kitchen. It was a slow, painful process as she left a snail trail of blood and fluids behind her. Her knees shook and her hands were numb. She could see them but not feel them very well. Her face was utterly numb and her scalp was hot. Sweat dripped down into her eyes, making them sting.

She stopped halfway down the short hallway to throw up. It was too much effort to go around the vomit, so she went through it. All she could focus on was the image in her mind. The cast iron griddle they used to make pancakes on lazy Saturday or Sunday mornings— when they had them.

She would heat that fucker up and then cauterize her wound.

Time to griddle your middle, Lady Vanity slyly joked.

That was funny. It hurt, but Frankie chuckled all the way down the hall to the kitchen.

The colossal effort of getting herself upright at the stove left her shaking. Her legs trembled like a newborn calf. The world wavered in and out of focus.

She put the griddle over the two power burners, turned them up full bloom, and waited.

The room grew warm and, eventually, she could feel the heat baking off the cast iron. She found two thick oven mitts and pulled them on.

Then, too tired to worry about it, she grabbed the griddle by both ends, turned the flat side toward herself, and pressed it to her midsection without hesitation.

All she could hear was her own screaming.

All she could smell was her cooking flesh.

The descent to the floor was rapid and painful.

She rapped her head on the edge of a stool.

She came to for just a second. Long enough to look down the length of her body. To relish the flatness she saw there. Black, red, blistered, and stinking.

But flat.

The next thing that came into view was the roof of a swaying ambulance (couldn't they turn off that fucking siren?) and Alex's pale face.

"I'm not done," she muttered. "Lady and I aren't done. Where are you taking me? I still have things to do. Touch ups."

"We're headed to—" he paused. "A plastic surgeon. For a consultation."

"Really?"

"Really."

She shut her eyes. "Thank you. You do love me."

"More than you'll ever know," he said in a garbled, far-off voice.

12

IT WAS THE BRIGHT LIGHT and scratchy voice that woke her. Her eyes were slits, her mouth was so dry it tasted like hot dirt. Her ears kept picking up a feedback noise and then it all swam into focus.

"Paging Doctor Griffith. Please call extension 42, Doctor Griffith . . ."

Her eyes shot open as it hit home. The roasted pork smell of her own burnt flesh still seemed to coat her nostrils. She tried to sit up but failed, hitting a tether—a leash?—partway up.

She jerked against it again and cried out.

Then Alex was at her side, looking down at her.

"Shh, shh. It's okay. Let me help you sit up."

Her head swam and she collapsed back against the overstuffed pillow. The pillowcase smelled like bleach and plastic.

Hospital.

She hated hospitals. She'd spent too much time in one when she was fourteen and her eating disorder was severe. She spent some time in another when she was a bit older, but that one wasn't for her body.

Oh God.

Her midsection was tender and numb at the same time. She looked down to see it swollen, distended. Her hands, where they stuck out from her wrists, were currently bound in padded cuffs that were connected to her bed rails.

"My stomach. Oh God. Was I wrong? Did I fail? It's so . . . *big.*"

Alex winced and looked alarmed at her remark. Then he bent slightly and the top of the bed started to rise up. He got her to a sitting position. Almost all the way, but she begged him to stop because it started to put pressure on her abdomen.

He pulled a chair closer and sat. "It's okay. It's fluids. From the surgery. You're just bloated. It'll all go down."

She sighed, something akin to relief settled in her chest like a small animal.

But then she wondered if he was telling the truth. If. He could be lying to her.

She tried to sit up straighter and pain lanced through her. She groaned.

"What's happening? Why are we here? You said you were taking me to a plastic surgeon."

He swallowed hard and nodded. "You eventually got to one. After they saved you from fucking dying. What were you thinking?" He squeezed her hand.

"I couldn't stand it, Alex. I had to fix it. I tried what Pastor Mike said, but I couldn't find any clothes. They were all so *hideous.* I was so hideous!"

"But you're not, hon. You're not. It was barely anything. The only person who noticed was you."

"I couldn't stand it," she repeated. "I fixed it. I found Lady and we fixed it. She helped me."

"Lady?"

She nodded. "Vanity. The knife."

He paled visibly and she wanted to laugh. To pat his hand and tell him it was fine. It was no big deal.

A short, round doctor waltzed in and beamed at her. "How are we feeling?"

"We're feeling chained up and restrained against our will," she replied. Alex leapt to his feet. "I want to go home," she said.

"We'll get to that eventually," the doctor said. His gaze strayed to Alex and she knew he was lying.

They were going to send her to the other hospital. They were going to "get her head on straight" the way they had once upon a time.

What they didn't understand was that for years—fucking years!—she'd been barely holding it together. Barely keeping herself acceptable to herself. Menopause had set its claws in despite her best efforts. Despite all her efforts!

She was breathing fast and the doctor leaned down. His eyes were surreally blue. The color of toilet water with those tabs in the tank.

"Do you need a paper bag?"

She couldn't stop. Her hands made fists, she jerked against the restraints. So hard something in her arm wrenched and she gasped. But she just kept going. She had no control over it.

He went to the door, called out for a nurse, and mumbled something to her.

The nurse bustled in, her pale blue scrubs whispering with every step. She smiled down at Frankie. A sad smile. A condescending smile.

She injected something in the line and said, "That'll help you feel better, honey."

Frankie opened her mouth to speak but, surprisingly fast, she felt a warm syrupy calm spread through her. She nodded. At what she had no idea.

The doctor and Alex were in conference. They kept darting worried glances at her. She heard specific words as if from far away.

Healing . . .

Evaluation . . .

Involuntary admission . . .

Dysmorphia . . .

Severe . . .

She shut her eyes for a moment. She was almost asleep when something was placed in her lap.

She opened her eyes to see a little pixyish redhead staring down at her, smiling.

"Your lunch, ma'am. If you'd like, I can put it over there if you'd rather nap."

Frankie was about to say yes to that offer, when her eyes roved the tray and she saw the plastic fork. The tines seemed to wink at her. She sat up straighter and hissed at the pain.

"What's that?" she asked.

The doctor and Alex were still in the corner comparing notes and plotting against her.

Her stomach ached. Her skin screamed. Her fingers and her feet were puffy. She felt inflated and disgusting and insanely uncomfortable.

"Salisbury steak," the girl said. She grinned. "I know it's not the most appetizing."

"Oh no, it's fine. I actually love Salisbury steak," Frankie said.

She studied the blip of pale white mashed potatoes, severely wilted green beans, a paper carton of apple juice and a bottle of water. A pre-packaged brownie sat at the edge of the tray.

The woman started to walk away, thinking Frankie had spaced out. And for good reason, she *had* fucking spaced out.

She tried to grab the girl's arm, forgetting the restraints for a second. When they caught, she gave an embarrassed laugh.

"I don't suppose you'd give me a knife, would you? To cut the steak?"

To cut and cut. Cutting can be fun!

The girl shook her head and gracefully looked regretful. "I'm sorry. There's a notice on the door. That's a non-metal fork or spoon only notice."

Frankie sighed. Her head was much clearer now that she was calm. After that lovely magical shot of whatever it had been.

She read the girl's little white name tag. "I understand, Melinda. Thank you, though."

The girl looked satisfied that she'd done all she could. She scooted past the men and left.

Frankie studied the fork. She slowly began to stab one green bean at a time.

She wanted Alex to explain to her what was going to happen. It was just rude to tell your trusting wife you were taking her to a plastic surgeon and then take her to the hospital. And get her—let's face it, folks—committed. Because that's what was coming.

All because she'd done a little self-improvement.

She ate her beans one at a time. Methodically.

He finally approached her looking worried and relieved all at once.

"What's going on? When can I go home?"

"First you have to heal," he said. He leaned against the side of the rail since he couldn't sit on the bed. "Then they need to evaluate you. You—that was insane. You cut off a big *piece* of yourself. A pretty fucking big piece."

She shrugged, chewing a bean between her front teeth. "It was extraneous. I didn't need it. We couldn't afford plastic surgery. I took care of it. The same way I've been taking care of things all these years. Weights, running, cardio, CrossFit."

He nodded along as if he understood.

"Honey, I picked a chunk of you up off the floor. I found you passed out holding a cast iron griddle. The burners were still burning like merry hell. You'd hit your head. You were . . . mutilated."

"It was an accident. I shouldn't have passed out."

"You shouldn't have carved yourself up like a roast!" he barked, startling her.

He rubbed his mouth with his fingers. "Sorry. I didn't mean to yell. I'm just—we're worried. We're all worried. We think it's best if you talk to someone before you go home."

She ran her finger up and down the tine of the fork. Then the shaft. The plastic was fairly thick.

She sat there wondering. Were there stitches under her bandages? There had to be stitches.

"I can talk to someone here. Please don't make me go to one of those places."

"Those places help people," he said. So sincere. So sure.

"They tell you you're fine. That it's in your head. That what you see isn't what other people see," she said. She choked on it. "But how could people not see how fucking gross I was? How fat and disgusting."

Her finger ran up and down the tine. Up and down. Then the handle. The handle would scrape fairly well. It had a blunt blade kind of feel to it.

The restraints left her just enough play to eat off the tray.

But that meant she could possibly reach the stitches. If they ever left her alone. If they ever crawled out of her ass.

And if the tines didn't work, they had to feed her again. Another fork. Maybe a spoon. Spoons could scoop! Another meal, another chance.

"Listen to me, Frankie. You are not fat. Or disgusting. And now you have to heal from the damage you did."

"The improvement," she corrected.

"The damage," he said, shaking her hand with anger.

She shook her head. "You don't understand."

"I don't. I do not understand. Not by a fucking longshot. But I do love you. And we'll get through this together."

What bullshit. He couldn't even see what she saw. How were they in this together? If they were in this together he'd have cauterized her so she wouldn't have fainted like a weak asshole.

She was in this alone.

But she nodded and smiled at him. "Okay. We'll figure it out. I want to be happy."

That was the most honest thing she'd ever said.

And she was so close. She just needed out of these cuffs and back home with Lady Vanity. The only understanding voice in her life.

They'd "fixed" her, but she could correct the damage they'd done. She was so close to her goal. Just a little more off the top. Maybe a little more off the sides.

She just had to play their game and wait.

In the meantime, she had the fork. She just needed a few minutes alone. Just to make a few modifications.

Just a few modifications and, eventually, she'd be perfect.

She would not go gently.

Ali Seay lives in Baltimore with her husband and kids and the ghost of a geriatric wiener dog who once ruled the house. She's the author of *Go Down Hard* (Grindhouse Press) and *To Offer Her Pleasure* (Weirdpunk Books). Her work can be found in numerous horror and crime anthologies. When not writing, she hunts vintage goods, rifles through used bookstores, and is always down for a road trip. For more info visit aliseay.com

Other Grindhouse Press Titles

#018__*The Last Porno Theater* by Nick Cato
#017__*Zombieville* by C.V. Hunt
#016__*Samurai Vs. Robo-Dick* by Steve Lowe
#015__*The Warm Glow of Happy Homes* by Andersen Prunty
#014__*How To Kill Yourself* by C.V. Hunt
#013__*Bury the Children in the Yard: Horror Stories* by Andersen Prunty
#012__*Return to Devil Town (Vampires in Devil Town Book Three)* by Wayne Hixon
#011__*Pray You Die Alone: Horror Stories* by Andersen Prunty
#010__*King of the Perverts* by Steve Lowe
#009__*Sunruined: Horror Stories* by Andersen Prunty
#008__*Bright Black Moon (Vampires in Devil Town Book Two)* by Wayne Hixon
#007__*Hi I'm a Social Disease: Horror Stories* by Andersen Prunty
#006__*A Life On Fire* by Chris Bowsman
#005__*The Sorrow King* by Andersen Prunty
#004__*The Brothers Crunk* by William Pauley III
#003__*The Horribles* by Nathaniel Lambert
#002__*Vampires in Devil Town* by Wayne Hixon
#001__*House of Fallen Trees* by Gina Ranalli
#000__*Morning is Dead* by Andersen Prunty